30天

雅思寫作7+攻略

必備句型 + 加分搭配詞 + 邏輯寫作大綱

取分重點考前完全掌握

蕭志億（派老師）著

考生見證

以下是準備雅思考生實際運用這本書中的 Task 1 攻略與 Task 2 **大綱式寫作**的心得分享，希望藉此讓讀者更加了解這個自創招式的威力與功效！

★ 張姓考生 寫作 7.0 ★

📍 考試地點：台北科技大學

✍ 考試成績：L7.5 R8 W7.0 S6.5 總分：7.5 分

🗓 考試日期：2017/11/11

寫作對我而言比較困難，因為已經一段時間沒有寫過完整的英文文章。小作文一開始看起來很難，因為我不擅長整理數據，但老師所給的方向，像是 **overall**、**上升或下降的趨勢**、**最大或最小值**等等都讓我可以有把握的在 20 甚至 15 分鐘內完成。相對來說，我一開始以為大作文是比較簡單的部分，到後來才發現要在短時間內，大量的運用不同單字、建構出邏輯關係，甚或要吸引考官閱讀是極其困難的。派老師整理出來的**寫作大綱**的確給了我很大的幫助。

★ 葉姓考生 寫作 7.0 ★

📍 考試地點：高雄恆逸訓練中心

✍ 考試成績：L9.0 S7.5 R8.0 W7.0，總分：8 分

🗓 考試日期：2020/03/29

小作文方面，我發現自己對整理數據、分項討論有很大的障礙，於是我開始分析老師發的佳作合集內的每一篇，再加上老師**改寫題目**、**overall**、**趨勢**、**數量公式**，最後考試時才穩定一些。小作文總是用掉我 20 至 25 分鐘的時間，因此在大作文方面我需要練習的就是速度，幸好有老師整理出的**大綱**，讓我考試的時候也能思緒清晰，不會因為緊張而拖慢速度。

📍 考試地點：北科集思會議中心

✍ 考試成績：L8.5 R9.0 W7.0 S8.0 總分：8.0 分

📅 考試日期：2019/10/12

對我而言，寫作也相當困難，畢竟自從高中畢業後就不曾用英文寫過任何一篇。派老師教的**大綱式寫作**在訓練時提供了很大的幫助，讓人很快掌握到寫作的基本概念。小作文方面，老師帶著我們解析各類型圖表的解讀方法，也教導了改寫的技巧，其中 collocation 是我對於英文這個領域從來都沒有的觀念，比起用生冷艱澀的難字，**動詞、名詞、形容詞的搭配得當**才是拿高分的關鍵，也更貼近母語人士的英文。最後老師的精選範例也提供非常大的幫助，在考試前的最後一個月，大量的從其中抓出**大綱**與用詞，在實戰時非常實用！

📍 考試地點：字神帝國北車

✍ 考試成績：L8 R7.5 W7.0 S7.0，總分：7.5 分

📅 考試日期：2020/09/12

派老師的寫作課是四科當中我收穫最多的一科，在小作文上老師教得很有系統，基本上照老師教的找出**最大／最小和趨勢**都不會有太大的問題。老師會分不同的圖表類型教，我自己最常練習常考的柱狀圖、折線圖和表格。而大作文是我覺得要花較多功夫練習的，我認為派老師教的讓步式寫法相當實用，正反論點都可以寫到，不會有論點不夠的問題，練習時我也會用老師教的**大綱式寫作**來整理論點以及補充的範文，規定自己一個禮拜要寫 2 ～ 3 個不同主題的文章來累積論點跟維持手感，才不會在正式考試遇到不熟的主題而寫不出論點，寫完再看範文，把好用的論點或優美的句型記下來。

自序

對於許多雅思考生而言，世界上最遙遠的距離，不是總分 7 分，而是**寫作 7 分**。

許多世界級名校，例如牛津、劍橋、倫敦大學、約翰·霍布金斯大學、墨爾本大學、雪梨大學等，除了要求考生總分必須達到其設定標準之外，常常**額外要求「寫作」單科不得低於 6.5 或 7 分**。這樣的要求讓許多學生望塵莫及……

你知道是什麼原因造成雅思寫作無法高分嗎？

一方面是因為寫作本來就不是一蹴可幾的能力，它必須是經年累月的實力養成，就像投三分球一樣，絕不是學到幾招之後，就可以馬上得心應手。

可是，大部分的考生，現實上，並沒有上述提到的「經年累月的時間」，培養出真正的寫作實力後，再去對付雅思。

另外一方面，很多考生對於**考試的評分標準**完全沒有概念，所以對於考官的喜好更是一知半解，或根本一竅不通。大部分考生可能都覺得寫作時的「**單字**」、「**文法**」是最重要的，但是卻不知道這兩項只是評分標準的其中兩點，還有更重要的「**文章內容**」以及「**文章邏輯**」。

當然，也有不少的學生遇到的問題是「沒有想法」，不知道該如何「說故事」或「清楚表達自己的看法」。只用「蜻蜓點水」的方式簡單描述，或用邏輯語意不清楚的方式在「創作」。

由於以上原因，常常陷入一種窘境，明明很認真上課，也很認真練習寫文章，甚至是瘋狂刷題了，但是分數卻一直停滯不前！

因此，《30 天雅思寫作 7+ 攻略》就應運而生了。寫此書目的就是希望幫助考生培養正確方式去戰勝雅思寫作，不僅在有限的時間內能夠考取高分，完成出國留學的夢想，進而幫助學生克服留學階段的各種寫作挑戰！

最後，我要勉勵各位考生，學習英文寫作就像是參加一場又一場的馬拉松運動，需要持之以恆，更要從失敗中學習教訓。從 5 公里、10 公里、半馬，到最後的全程馬拉松，應戰雅思也是如此。

在這裡送上我在上課時常用來勉勵學生的一段話，希望鼓勵各位同學們能夠順利考取理想分數。

I, ＿＿＿＿＿＿＿＿＿＿＿＿＿, strongly believe I can conquer English, transcend my limitation, and finally, fulfill my dream.

No matter how challenging it will be in the near future, I know I can do it.

空格請填上自己的名字，表示對自己的學習負責！

字神帝國英語學院英文講師

派老師／Patrick

目次

CHAPTER 1
雅思寫作評分標準與範例

CHAPTER 2
Task1 圖表寫作／書信

CHAPTER 3
你不知道的加分祕密：詞語搭配（Collocation）

CHAPTER 4
Task 2 學術寫作

CHAPTER 5

再多 7 天，讓你提升到 Band 7 的加分句型

雅思寫作考試類型

A 學術組 vs. 一般訓練組

雅思寫作主要分兩種：學術組（Academic）和一般組（General Training），兩種類型的題型有分別，下方圖表為兩種類型的比較。目前雅思考生學術組需求多，題型上也因為要應付學術能力需求，更為複雜，因此本書會著重在學術組的寫作類型。

IELTS Writing	對象	題型
學術組	**留學**申請	Task 1 **圖表**寫作 & Task 2 申論寫作
一般組	**移民**申請	Task 1 **書信**寫作 & Task 2 申論寫作

B 紙筆測驗 vs. 電腦測驗

這兩種測驗方式的考試頻率（紙筆為 4 場／月；電腦為每週每天都可考）、報名時間（紙筆為最晚考前 1 週；電腦則是最晚考前 3 天）、成績公布（紙筆為考後 13 天；電腦則是考後 5 到 7 天）皆不同。而寫作的差異則如下表：

IELTS Writing	紙筆測驗	電腦測驗
注意事項	1. 字跡勿過於潦草 2. 修改時注意版面	1. 修改較容易 2. 有字數統計
如何選擇	如打字速度快，可選擇電腦測驗 但以平常練習時為主的方式最為適合	

老師提醒

考試就像打仗，必須要知己知彼，才能百戰百勝。熟悉選擇的考試類型，以及了解考試當天的注意事項，才不會在考試當天出錯，導致表現失常甚至無法順利考試，這樣真的是得不償失。

CHAPTER

1

雅思寫作評分標準與範例

1.1

寫作評分四大標準
了解考官喜好，才能投其所好

雅思寫作第一個常見的問題是，考生根本搞不清楚考官要的東西是什麼，誤以為只要寫出高級的單字、高級的句型、文法錯誤不要太多，這樣就會高分了。殊不知這只是評分標準中的一小部分而已。

這樣做就會很像你對待另外一半時，她明明很喜歡花，但你自以為她喜歡巧克力，然後就瘋狂買很多巧克力給她吃，結果換來一頓罵，更糟糕的是，你還搞不清楚為何會挨罵，明明這麼努力去找尋了很多特殊口味的巧克力，用了很多心力，但是卻不被讚賞。真正原因是因為對於另外一半來說，吃太多巧克力反而容易胖，她要的是一種浪漫，所以才希望對方送她花。

因此，想要雅思寫作得高分，就要先搞清楚考官在意的事情是什麼，不是你自己一廂情願的想法。接下來，我們來好好了解如何投其所好。

雅思寫作評分

雅思寫作測驗分為 2 大部分進行撰寫，在下列 4 項評分標準中，會出現特別看重的部分：

(1)	Task 1: Task Achievement Task 2: Task Response	文意準確性與回答內容 (TA/TR)
(2)	Coherence and Cohesion	語意連貫度 (CC)
(3)	Lexical Resource	詞彙豐富度 (LR)
(4)	Grammatical Range and Accuracy	文法掌握度 (GRA)

1. Task 1 和 Task 2 將會分開計算，考生將會得到每一項目的分數，加總後再除於 4。**單科不會四捨五入，而是無條件式捨去。**

Task 1	TA	CC	LR	GRA	Total ÷ 4
	8	8	7	7	30 ÷ 4 = **7.5**

Task 2	TA	CC	LR	GRA	Total ÷ 4
	7	7	7	6	26 ÷ 4 = 6.75 → **6.5**

2. **最後 Task 1 和 Task 2 再加總起來，四捨五入後，才是寫作的真正分數。** 例如：

總分計算方式：$(\text{Task 1} \times 1 \div 3) + (\text{Task 2} \times 2 \div 3)$

$(7.5 \times 1 \div 3) + (6.5 \times 2 \div 3) = 6.83 \rightarrow \textbf{7.0}$

(1) Task Achievement/Response

這項評分標準主要是針對你是否回答題目、主要觀點以及你如何論證它們。

要提升這項分數，你需要：

√ 用相關的論點去回答題目。

√ 整篇文章的立場很清楚。

√ 清楚寫出支持論點，且沒有離題。

√ 至少寫超過 150 個字（Task 1）／ 250 個字（Task 2）。

犯了以下錯誤，會嚴重扣分：

× 只有部分回答題目的問題。

× 想法太過於廣泛，只有簡單回答題目，沒有具體的內容去支持論點。

× 出現不相關或離題的內容。

(2) Coherence and Cohesion

考官會檢查文章的結構、分段以及連接詞（過渡詞）的使用。

要提升這項分數，你需要：

√ 寫四或五段，意思是你應該要寫兩到三段中間段落。

√ 每一個中間段落都只有一個主題。

√ 語意非常有邏輯。

√ 運用各種過渡詞。

√ 避免錯誤使用過渡詞。

犯了以下錯誤，會嚴重扣分：

✕ 組織：想法不清楚或邏輯不清。

✕ 過渡詞：使用太多過渡詞，而且總是在每個句子的開頭。

✕ 分段：有太多或太少段落，而且有些段落只有一個句子。

✕ 中心思想：每一個段落沒有一個清楚的中心思想或主題句。

(3) Lexical Resource

考官會檢查單字使用、拼錯字、錯誤數量。

要提升這項分數，你需要：

√ 善用詞語搭配，尤其是動詞加名詞的組合。

√ 單字有變化而且很正確。

√ 避免使用口語單字。

√ 拼字正確。

犯了以下錯誤，會嚴重扣分：

✕ 單字變化不夠，不足以去討論或延伸內容。

✕ 單字選擇不夠精準或是不正確的單字使用。

✕ 使用不常見的單字，老生常談或是諺語過度使用，單字選擇不適當，例如 henceforth（從現在開始）。或是非正式的用字，例如 gonna。

✕ 拼字太多明顯錯誤，而且影響到考官理解。

×出現詞性錯誤，例如 I am unemployment.

（原句 employment 為名詞，應改成形容詞 unemployed。）

(4)　Grammatical Range and Accuracy

考官會檢查你的句子結構，時態、文法以及錯誤數量。

要提升這項分數，你需要：

√ 注意句子結構。

√ 使用不同的句型。

√ 使用正確的標點符號。

√ 避免文法錯誤，常見錯誤：冠詞、複數名詞、不可數名詞。

√ 轉換不同文法時態。

犯了以下錯誤，會嚴重扣分：

×句型變化不夠，使用不同句型來表達內容。

×出現太多錯誤的句子。

×標點符號有一些錯誤。標點符號要精準，避免大小寫、逗號和句號錯誤。

 老師提醒

記住，想要掌握高分關鍵，首先要抓住考官的心，也就是要非常清楚了解考官的評分標準。相反地，只是一味地寫出很多漂亮單字，但是整篇文章的前後語意邏輯不清楚，寫作論點非常膚淺，甚至是寫出錯誤的單字用法，這樣是無法得到高分的喔！

1.2

學術組 Task 1 範例與考官評分／評語

(WRITING TASK 1)

You should spend about 20 minutes on this task.

> *The chart below shows the results of a survey about people's coffee and tea buying and drinking habits in five British cities.*
>
> *Summarise the information by selecting and reporting the main features, and make comparisons where relevant.*

Write at least 150 words.

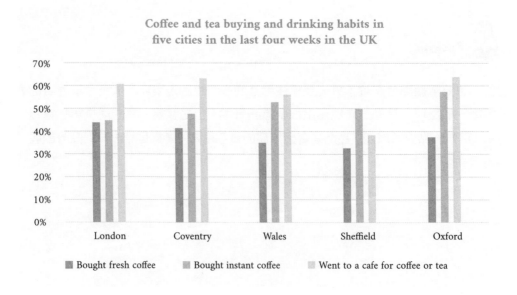

This is an answer written by a candidate who achieved a **Band 6.0** score.

範文

The bar chart depicts the outcomes of a questionare of how often people buy and drink different types of coffee in London, Coventry, Wales, Sheffield, and Oxford of the UK.

The first option is bought fresh coffee in last 4 weeks. In London has 43.5% of city residents and has amost the same amount as Coventry which is 42.3%. Wales and Sheffield have a nearly same amount, 34.3% and 34.5 %. Next, Oxford has 38.5%.

The second line is bought instant coffee in last 4 weeks. Wales has 52.5%. Other two cities that have amost the same number are Sheffield, 49.7%, and Coventry, 48.5%. The lowest number is 45.5% of London and the highest number is 54.2% of Oxford.

The last option of the survey shows the percentage of city residents that went to a café for coffee or tea in last 4 weeks. In London, people went to a café for coffee or tea in last 4 weeks 62% of city residents. In Wales, citizens went to a café for coffee or tea in last 4 weeks 55.3%. The lowest is Sheffield that shows 49.8% of city residents. In Oxford, people went to a café for coffee or tea in last 4 weeks 62.8%. The highest is Coventry that shows 63.5%.

In conclusion, the highest number of the survey is the percentage of city residents that went to a café for coffee or tea in last 4 weeks because it shows almost the highest percentage in three types. (249 words)

考官評語

[1]This answer covers most relevant information in the task, and clearly highlights the main trends and comparisons. Accurate data are used to support his/her description. [2]Organisation is clear, including introduction and overview, one paragraph per category. The information is clearly linked across the whole answer due to the use of cohesive devices [*The first option* / *The second line* / *The last option*]. [3] Despite occasional errors [questionare / questionnaire, amost / almost], vocabulary is adequate and appropriate for the task. [4]Grammar shows a combination of simple and complex sentence structures with a certain level of accuracy. A wide range of vocabulary and/or grammatical range also help to improve the score.

翻譯

[1] 這篇文章涵蓋了大部分相關的內容,並且清楚凸顯出主要趨勢與比較。這些描述有精確的資料來佐證。[2] 文章結構是清楚的,包括開頭介紹、整體趨勢,一段一個項目。整篇文章的資訊連貫很清楚,因為有使用連接用語(第一個選項／第二條線／最後一個選項)。[3] 單字表達整體上是充分且適當的,雖然偶有一些錯誤(questionare / questionnaire, amost / almost)。[4] 文法包括正確的簡單句和複雜句。單字變化和文法句型變化很多,也有加分作用。

評語講解

第 1 句是評分標準中的 Task Achievement
第 2 句是評分標準中的 Coherence and Cohesion
第 3 句是評分標準中的 Lexical Resource
第 4 句是評分標準中的 Grammatical Range and Accuracy

1.3

一般組 Task 1 範例與考官評分／評語

(WRITING TASK 1)

You should spend about 20 minutes on this task.

> *A friend of yours is thinking about applying for the same course that you did at university. He/She has asked for your advice about studying this subject.*
>
> *Write a letter to your friend. In your letter*
> * *give details of the course you took at the university*
> * *explain why you recommend the university*
> * *give some advice about how to apply*

Write at least 150 words.

You do **NOT** need to write any addresses.

Begin your letter as follows:

Dear ... ,

This is an answer written by a candidate who achieved a **Band 7.0** score.

Dear William,

I hope this letter finds you well.

As per your request, with regard to advice, I am writing to you so you can gain some more information about the course, the university and the application process.

First of all, the course I studied was Intensive English, offered either in the morning or the evening. The one in the morning starts from 7 to 11am Monday to Thursday; on the other hand, the one in the evening is from 5 to 9pm on the same days. The whole course lasts 10 weeks. They are always taught by the brilliant teachers. That's really motivating.

Secondly, the university is so organized! Besides, it's in your neighborhood so access is easy. The tuition is something you can afford and they give you different options. The university really cares about your learning process so they also offer a tutor to help you if needed. I really recommend you the institution.

In order to complete the application, you just have to call the number of registration office and the receptionist will ask you for the course code, whic is 165, and some personal details. He'll let you know when the course begin.

I hope you find it useful! Do not hesitate to contact me again.

Regards, Jean

(211 words)

考官評語

[1]This letter covers all thee bullet points to some extent, with well-developed ideas and extended description for each bullet point. [2]Information is clearly and logically organized due to a clear progression throughout the script. Cohesive devices are used appropriately [*First of all* | *Besides* | *In order to*] and there is use of reference [*They*] and substitution [*The one in the morning* | *the one in the evening* | *the same days.*] [3]There is evidence of less common vocabulary [*motivating* | *access* | *learning process* | *institution* | *receptionist*] and there are only occasional spelling errors [*whic* | *which*]. [4]A variety of complex structures are used, showing a high level of grammatical control.

翻譯

[1] 這封信在一定程度上涵蓋了所有要點，因為每個要點的想法都有拓展和延伸的描述。[2] 資訊清楚且有邏輯地排列，整篇文章有一個清晰的進展。連接詞語使用恰當（*First of all* | *Besides* | *In order to*），而且有使用代名詞（They）以及指代關係詞做代換（*The one in the morning* | *the one in the evening* | *the same days*）。[3] 有一些比較少見的用字（*motivating* | *access* | *learning process* | *institution* | *receptionist*），而且只有一些拼字錯誤（*whic* | *which*）。[4] 有很多複雜句子，表示考生對文法的掌控能力佳。

評語講解

第 1 句是評分標準中的 Task Achievement
第 2 句是評分標準中的 Coherence and Cohesion
第 3 句是評分標準中的 Lexical Resource
第 4 句是評分標準中的 Grammatical Range and Accuracy

1.4

學術組 Task 2 範例與考官評分／評語

In some countries, owning a home rather than renting one is very important for people.

Why is this the case?
Do you think this is a positive or negative situation?

考官評語

This is an answer written by a candidate who achieved a **Band 7.0** score.

範文

In some countries, the ownership of people's home is important. In these countries it is of critical importance to own your own home rather than renting it. It might be indifferent for some, but for these people it matters.

First of all, owning your own home is crucial because your home is supposed to be exactly what is sounds like: a sweet home. As a human, we long after having stuff to call it our own, but doesn't matter what it is because humans will always want to claim ownership. This is nothing different and new and it has always been like this through human history. Colonies, for example, later once again became the same country before led by its own inhabitants. People will always want to be the one who decides what happens to them; however, if you rent your home, you can't even paint it without the owners permission.

If you are rent an apartment, there might be a lot of stresses in your life. A scratched wall can cause you a major headache because the wall does not belong to you. The bedroom you are sleeping in might not be available as long as you hope. Things happen in life and maybe the next landlord won't want to have you as a tenant.

On the other hand, not owning your home could be a relief when it comes to your finance. As a renter, you won't have to be responsible for mortgage, loans or an awful lot of money on buying the property. You wouldn't have to worry that the house market may crash or a natural disaster may destroy your luxurious, fancy home.

In conclusion, I think I would rather own my house need to have a home and calling it your own can make that more special. (302 words)

心得筆記

考官評語

[1]The candidate clearly explains why home ownership may extremely important to some people, and also explores the advantages and disadvantages of owning your own home before expressing his or her own opinion. The task is well addressed and ideass are explored in certain depth. [2]Organisation is clear due to a good use of cohesive devices. Paragraphing and the message is also easy to follow. [3]The range of vocabulary is appropriate, with examples of less common vocabulary [*long after / for / house / housing market*] and good use of collocations [*claim ownership / a major headache / pay mortgage / natural disaster*]. [4]There is a variety of complex sentence structures, with a good level of accuracy, albeit a minor error [*owners / owner's*].

翻譯

[1] 考生清楚解釋為何擁有家對於某些人是很重要的。另外，在提出她／他自己真正的立場前，探討了擁有自己家的正方和反方論點。文章有確實回答題目，內容探討也很有深度。[2] 文章組織結構很清楚，運用了連接用語和清楚分段，所以文章很好閱讀。[3] 單字變化很充分，而且有使用到一般考生比較少用到的單字 (long after / for / house / housing marekt) 以及好的詞語搭配 (claim ownership / a major headache / pay mortgage / natural disaster)。[4] 有很多複雜句構的變化，而且非常正確，雖然有一些小錯誤（owners / owner's）。

評語講解

第 1 句是評分標準中的 Task Response
第 2 句是評分標準中的 Coherence and Cohesion
第 3 句是評分標準中的 Lexical Resource
第 4 句是評分標準中的 Grammatical Range and Accuracy

CHAPTER
2

Task1 圖表寫作／書信

2.1

學術組：Task 1 常考的六種題型

Task 1 的必考類型有 6 種：

1.	37%	Bar chart	（柱狀圖）
2.	23%	Line graph	（曲線圖）
3.	16%	Table	（表格）
4.	14%	Map	（地圖題）
5.	5%	Pie chart	（圓餅圖）
6.	5%	Flow chart	（流程圖）

依上方數據，**Bar chart （柱狀圖）** 是最常考的題型，再來依序是 Line graph （曲線圖）、Table（表格）、Map（地圖題）、Pie chart（圓餅圖），而 Flow chart （流程圖）是出題機率最低的題型，但是為了避免考試中還是遇見它，後面題型解析還是會教你如何完成 Flow chart 喔！

每次考試要寫其中一種圖形，或是兩種圖片的混合題，例如 Line graph （曲線圖）加 Table（表格）。總字數至少要寫 150 個字，考官會真的去算字數，如果低於 150 個字，會扣分。注意，盡量在 20 分鐘內要寫完，因為寫作考試時間總共只有一個小時，要完成 Task 1 + Task 2。因此，剩下的 40 分鐘要留給第二篇作文，因為 Task 2 的配分是佔寫作總分的 2/3。

2.2

學術組：寫出四段文章、一一擊破

考試時，建議只花 20 分鐘來完成 Task 1，因此如何正確分段是得分關鍵。文章結構分成四段，考官就很容易能看懂整篇文章的內容與重點。如果分段清楚的話，對於評分標準中的 Coherence and Cohesion 會有加分作用。建議每段各 5 分鐘。

四段文章

| 1. 改寫題目 | 2. 整體趨勢 | 3. 重要細節 | 4. 重要細節 |

1. 第一段：分析題目 + 改寫題目

分析完題目後，第一步驟就是開始改寫文字題目，再加上圖表中的資訊，即可完成第一段。完成後，開始分析圖表內容，找出哪裡有 compare 和 contrast 的細節。總長時間不能超過 5 分鐘，否則後面的時間就會被拖累到。

第一段就是改寫題目，聽起來很簡單，但是，實際上該怎麼寫才是最簡單也是最容易得分的寫法是哪一個呢？

a. We can see that the graph showed information on the number of sales of two types of coffee in ten years.

b. **The chart illustrates the number of sales of two types of coffee (Latte and Cappuccino) between 2000 and 2010.**

Answer

b 的寫法才是最正確的，因為第一句話使用了比較口語的單字，例如 We can see that，而且沒有寫到具體的咖啡類型（Latte and Cappuccino）和時間長度（between 2000 and 2010）。

2. 第二段：整體趨勢

上一步驟分析完圖片後，表示已經找到圖片中最重要的整體趨勢是什麼，用 1-2 句話的長度來完成第二段整體趨勢。此時的內容不會寫到具體的數據，只會描述到**最大、最小、上升、下降**的情況。

官方釋放出來的雅思寫作評分標準表中，上面就清楚寫到這句話，如果要得到 7 分的話，必須要 **present a clear overview of main trends, differences or stages**。注意，整體趨勢是 Task 1 的關鍵，因為考官會特地去尋找考生的答案中是否包含這項重要資訊，因為整體趨勢的內容要描述到圖表中重要的資訊，包括**最大、最小、上升、下降**的資訊，而且還要想辦法去 compare 和 contrast。

特別注意 2.3 的 **11 種 Task 1 常見錯誤**中的 **(2) 沒有 compare 和 contrast** 和 **(3) 沒有整體趨勢**，也是第二段要特別注意會被扣分的情況。

3. 第三 + 四段：中間段落要說明圖表中最重要的細節

Summarise the information by selecting and reporting the **main features**, and **make comparisons** where relevant.

上述這段英文是考題中的說明，請注意第一句話，考官清楚說明考生要 **select and report main features**，也就是第三、四段就是要把圖片中最重要的資訊找出來。想要做到這項要求，考生必須加上具體的數據和年代，清楚地描述出圖表中的重要細節。此時如果單字和句型能夠清楚呈現內容，而且也富有變化，想要拿到 7 分，不是夢想。

此外，上述英文的第二句話中，清楚說明要考生 **make comparisons**，也就是考生要能夠分析出圖表中的內容，哪裡有**類似的內容（compare）**，哪裡有**相對的內容（contrast）**，並且用出正確的單字與句型呈現出來。

2.3

11 種 Task 1 的常見錯誤

以下是雅思寫作 Task 1 的常見錯誤，想要得高分就必須先避免這些錯誤喔！

1. 時間分配錯誤

雅思寫作的時間總長是 1 小時，考生必須在考試時間內完成兩種不同類型的寫作：Task 1 圖表寫作 + Task 2 學術寫作，各一篇。寫作順序或長度由考生自行決定，但是通常都會**建議 Task 在 20 分鐘以內要完成（至少要寫 150 個字）。剩下的 40 分鐘則用來完成 Task 2 （至少要寫 250 個字）**，因為兩種寫作的配分不一樣。Task 1 佔總分 1/3，而 Task 2 佔總分 2/3。

如果考生無法使用上述的時間分配策略來作答的話，強烈建議先寫 Task 2，寫完後剩下的時間再完成 Task 1，因為即使 Task 1 沒有寫完，被扣分的比例也比較小。

2. 沒有 compare 和 contrast

Task 1 最重要的內容就是考官希望考生能夠分析出圖表中的內容，**哪裡有類似的內容（compare），哪裡有相對的內容（contrast）**，並且用出正確的單字與句型呈現出來。比較看看下面哪一句才有 compare 或 contrast。

a. School A shows a sharp upward trend in enrolments from $25 to $100 thousand from 2000 to 2005. School B has a minimal rise from $20 to $30 thousand over the same period.

b. From 2000 to 2005, School A shows a sharp upward trend in enrolments, **while** school B has a minimal rise, from $25 to $100 thousand and $20 to $30 thousand respectively.

正確答案是 b，因為 a 的句子只是分開描述出兩個資訊，**但是 b 用了對比句型 while**

去呈現出 school A 和 B 是相反的情況，一個是下降，另一個是上升。這樣的句子才會有加分作用。

3. 沒有整體趨勢

這一點是 Task 1 的致命傷，因為考官會特地去尋找考生的答案中是否包含這項重要資訊，因為整體趨勢的內容要描述到圖表中重要的資訊，包括最大、最小、上升、下降的資訊，而且還要想辦法去 compare 和 contrast。如果你仔細去看官方釋放出來的雅思寫作評分標準表的話，就會發現上面清楚寫到這句話，如果要得到 7 分的話，必須要 **present a clear overview of main trends, differences or stages**，如接下來的例子：

Overall, the number of burglary **declined** significantly from 2003 to 2012, while that of car theft **rose** steadily over the same period. Also, the figure of robbery **remained stable** between 2003 and 2012.

這句話描述了三條線的**下降**、**上升**以及持平的情況。而且第一句中用了 while 這個對比句型來呈現，會有加分作用。

4. 多寫了結尾段

請不要再多一段結尾段來結束你的文章，因為整體趨勢已經包含全部重要的內容了，如果再多寫一段結尾段，到最後就會變成**重複內容**了。

此外，寫了結尾段不僅僅重複內容，甚至可能更糟糕的是，**把兩個重要的整體趨勢，放在不同的位置**，一個在整體趨勢，另一個在結尾段，這樣會影響 coherence 和 cohesion 的評分，因為已經影響考官看整篇文章的理解了。

5. 描述不夠精準

在描述資料時，如果圖表中的資料沒有在明確的時間點或數據上面時，要再加上類

似 **about** 這樣的用字，否則也會算是描述不夠精準喔！

You should spend about 20 minutes on this task.

> *The chart below shows the total number of minutes (in billions) of telephone cells in the US, divided into three categories, from 2000-2007.*
>
> *Summarise the information by selecting and reporting the main features, and make comparisons where relevant.*

Write at least 150 words.

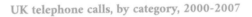

UK telephone calls, by category, 2000-2007

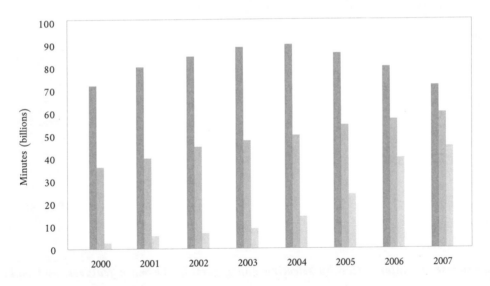

- Local calls
- National and international calls
- Mobiles calls

描述不精準：

Minutes spent on local calls fluctuated over the time period, with 70 billion minutes in 2000, peaking at 90 billion in 2004 and then gradually dropping to 70 billion minutes in 2007.

加上粗體字，就會比較精準一點：

Minutes spent on local calls fluctuated over the time period, with **just over** 70 billion minutes in 2000, peaking at **approximately** 90 billion in 2004 and then gradually dropping to **just under** 70 billion minutes in 2007.

其他參考單字：
* 低於某個數值

(just / slightly /well) under = below = less than

* 接近某個數值。

about = approximately = around = almost = roughly = nearly = close to

* 高於某個數值。

(just / slightly) over = above = more than

6. 避免寫出流水帳

千萬不要一五一十地描述全部的內容，這不是考官想要看到的內容。下面這句話，是考題中會出現的句子，已經清楚說明考試的遊戲規則了。

Summarise the information by selecting and reporting the main features, and make comparisons where relevant.

Writing Tasking 1

You should spend about 20 minutes on this task.

> *The bar chart below shows the top ten countries for the production and consumption of electricity in 2019.*
>
> *Summarise the information by selecting and reporting the main features, and make comparisons where relevant.*

Write at least 150 words

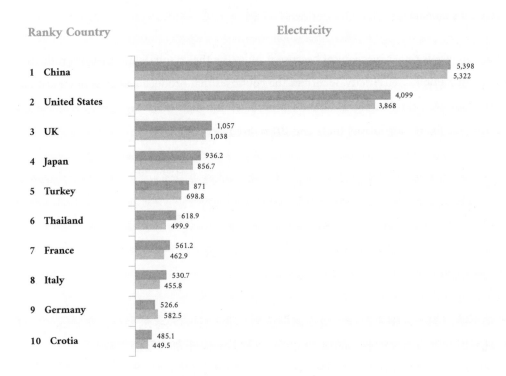

Ranky Country　　　　　　　　　Electricity

Rank	Country	Production (billion kWh)	Consumption (billion kWh)
1	China	5,398	5,322
2	United States	4,099	3,868
3	UK	1,057	1,038
4	Japan	936.2	856.7
5	Turkey	871	698.8
6	Thailand	618.9	499.9
7	France	561.2	462.9
8	Italy	530.7	455.8
9	Germany	526.6	582.5
10	Crotia	485.1	449.5

▪ Production (billion kWh)　　▪ Consumption (billion kWh)

From the bar chart that show the top ten countries for the production and consumption of electricity in 2019. For the production of electricity, the 1st rank is China that have 5,398 billion kwh, the 2nd rank is United States that have 4,099 billion kwh, the 3rd rank is the UK that have 1,059 billion kwh, the 4th rank is Japan that have 936.2 billion kwh, the 5th rank is Turkey that have 891 billion kwh, the 6th rank is Thailand that have 618.9 billion kwh, the 7th rank is France that have 561.2 billion kwh, the 8th rank is Italy that have 530.9 billion kwh, the 9th rank is Germany that have 526.6 billion kwh and the 10th rank is Croatia that have 485.1 billion kwh.

我們來看看考官的評語與評分：

This is an answer written by a candidate who achieved a **Band 5.0** score. Here is the examiner's comment:

This response is rather mechanical because it only lists the countries in order of production and consumption of electricity, identifies the countries that produce and consume most and least... However, the writing is supported by data, although there are some errors in the figures (the figures for Russia, India and Brazil are inaccurate.) ...

考官指出，考生只是機械式列出圖片中的資料，而且還出現了低級錯誤，連數據都抄錯。因此，再次強調，你只要寫出有 compare 和 contrast 的細節即可，才不會浪費太多時間寫出沒有意義的內容，而且又耽誤了 Task 2 的時間，真是賠了夫人又折兵。

7. 要忘記自我

千萬不要用第一人稱來寫作，也不需要去解讀圖表中的內容是因為什麼原因。只要單純寫出你分析出來的重點即可。因此，下面的句型**千萬不要使用**喔！

× In my opinion...

× I believe that...

× I think that...

× I would suggest...

× therefore/thus/thereby/hence

× because/for/as/since

× due to/because of/owing to

8. 時態錯誤

Task 1 到底要寫什麼時態呢？這也是考生常常搞不清楚的狀況，然後糊里糊塗就被扣分了。常見情況下的正確寫法有四種：

1) 題目沒有給日期：現在式
E.g. Britain **produces** 5% of the world's carbon dioxides emissions—about the same as India, which **has** five times as many people.

2) 題目給過去日期：過去式
E.g. **In 2002**, over 70% of respondents with annual incomes above $500,000 **considered** leisure time extremely or very important.

3) 題目給未來日期：未來式
E.g. The total US greenhouse gas emissions **will/are projected/predicted to** rise by 34% **from 2000 to 2030**.

E.g. **It is predicted that** the number of people committing violent crime is likely to rise by **the end of 2025**.

4) 題目包含過去到未來的日期：過去式和未來式
E.g. **In 2010**, the number of sales **stood** at 4 million and **will/is forecast to** rise to a peak of 11 million **by 2040**.

9. 單字句型沒有變化

別忘記了，評分重點中有兩項是在**評分單字和句型的變化**：Lexical resource 和 Grammar range and accuracy。看看下面的範例，用詞性變化是最簡單也是最有變化的一種方式喔！

a. The number of cases of pneumonia **increased steadily** from 30 to 55 in the first five years.

b. There was **a steady rise** in the number of cases of pneumonia to reach 55 in 1987 from 30 in the first five years.

說明：b 的單字和句型都做了變化，因為 b 把動詞 increased 轉變成 rise，把副詞 steadily 變成形容詞 steady，而且也把句型轉變成 there was 的用法，也讓 rise 轉變成名詞的用法。

在描述趨勢時，還有以下各種代換用法：

上升
rise / increase / climb / grow / go up / jump / rocket / soar / escalate

下降
drop / fall / decline / decrease / plunge / plummet / go down

最高點
peak at / reach a peak of / hit a high of

最低點
bottom out / hit the bottom of / hit a low of

持平
remain constant / keep steady / stay stable / level off

如果要加上變化程度的話，有以下形容詞或副詞可選擇。

變化程度大
sharp (ly) / quick (ly) / rapid (ly) / steep (ly) / significant (ly) / considerable / considerably / substantial (ly) / dramatic (ally) / drastic (ally)

變化程度小
gradual(ly) / steady / steadily / moderate(ly) / slight(ly) / slow(ly) / gentle / gently / little by little (adv.) / step by step (adv.)

10. 文法錯誤

雅思寫作中常見的錯誤如下，考生可以在寫作過程中檢查這些項目。

- 冠詞（a／an／the）
- 單複數
- 詞性變化
- 可數／不可數名詞
- 標點符號（常見為逗號和句號）
- 動詞時態
- 介系詞
- 主詞動詞一致性（第三人稱動詞變化）
- 指稱錯誤

以下句子皆有常見文法錯誤，試著找出錯誤並改正

a. While the spending on housing was 42% in 2015 the spending was 25% in 2018.

b. The pie charts shows the typical expenses of a household in five categories.

c. There was significantly decrease in spending on housing from 55% to 25%.

d. The spending on coffee is 13% in 1960 and 33% in 1980.

e. The least amount spent in 2000 was in health care.

f. There were 100,000 people work full-time in 2004 than in 1994.

g. The figures of commuters traveling by car and train both experience a steady increase during a period of sixty years. While, the figure of those who travel by bus falls slightly.

h. Australia was lower, at 15 million tonnes of wheat exports.

✕ 錯誤解析

a. While the spending on housing was 42% in 2015, the spending was 25%.

說明：標點符號的錯誤，此句雖然只少了逗號，但是會讓前後的子句斷句不清楚，混淆讀者的閱讀理解力。

b. The pie charts **show** the typical expenses of a household in five categories.
說明：主詞動詞一致性的錯誤。

c. There was **a significant decrease** in spending on housing from 55% to 25%.
說明：詞性的錯誤，此時的 decrease 是可數名詞，所以前面要有一個冠詞 a，而且只能用形容詞 significant 去修飾它。

d. The spending on coffee **was** 13% in 1960 and 33% in 1980.
說明：時態錯誤。

e. The least amount spent in 2000 was **on** health care.
說明：介系詞錯誤，此時要用 on 是因為前面的動詞是 spend。

f. There were 100,000 people **working** full-time in 2004 than in 1994.
說明：這是雙動詞的錯誤，前面已經有 be 動詞 were 了，後面又加上 work，這就是錯誤的。改成現在分詞 working 就沒問題了。

g. The figures of commuters traveling by car and train both experience a steady increase during a period of sixty years, **while** the figure of those who travel by bus falls slightly.
說明：這是 sentence fragment（不完整句子）的錯誤，因為 while 是連接詞，一定要連接兩個句子。把句號改成逗號，再把 while 改成小寫，就可以連接兩個句子了。

h. **The number of** Australia was lower, at 15 million tonnes of wheat exports.
說明：這是主詞描述錯誤的類型，如果少了 the number of 的話，就會變成「澳洲比較低」，很像澳洲可以移動一樣。所以要加上 the number of 才是正確的描述方式，表示「澳洲……的數量比較低」。

以下提供更多描述時間（時間長度可代換）的變化句型

from... to...	從……到……
between... and...	在……到……之間
over the next XX months / years / period	在接下來的 XX 個月 / 年 / 期間
in the following XX years	在接下來的 XX 年
at the beginning / end of the period	在此期間的開始 / 結束
three years later	三年後
in the first / last (final) year	在頭一年 / 最後一年

11. 不熟悉評分標準

考官評分的標準有下列四個項目，每個項目都會給分數，加總後除於四，就是寫作的分數。

Task Achievement	(25%)	文意準確性與回答內容
Coherence and Cohesion	(25%)	語意連貫度
Vocabulary	(25%)	詞彙豐富度
Grammatical Range and Accuracy	(25%)	文法掌握度

了解考官的評分標準讓你可以真正了解考試的重點，也就是說當你在寫作時，該著重的內容是什麼，不是一味地寫出很多漂亮單字而已。

 老師提醒

記住，一定要熟練 Task 1 之後再上考場，否則很難在 20 分鐘內完成，進而拖累到 Task 2 的作答時間，這樣可是得不償失，因為 Task 2 的比重佔總分的 2/3 喔！

2-4

學術組：三天搞定 Task 1
Day 1　Bar chart

(Writing Task 1)

You should spend about 20 minutes on this task.

> *The chart below shows the results of a survey about people's coffee and tea buying and drinking habits in five British cities.*
>
> *Summaries the information by selecting and reporting the main features, and make comparisons where relevant.*

Write at least 150 words.

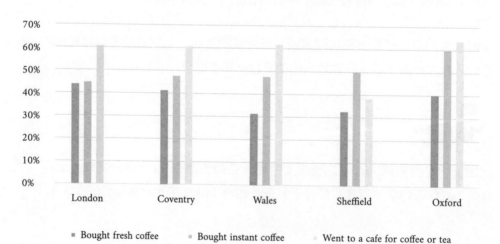

Coffee and tea buying and drinking habits in
five cities in the last four weeks in the UK

四段文章

第一段	第二段	第三段	第四段
改寫題目	整體趨勢	重要細節	重要細節

 老師提醒

此圖形是 Task 1 最常見的考題，一定要熟練此圖形後再上場考試。

高分範文

The bar chart exhibits the percentages of residents' habits of coffee and tea purchase and consumption over the last four weeks in five different cities (London, Coventry, Wales, Sheffield, and Oxford) in the UK.

Overall, it is obvious that going to a café for coffee or tea was the most common, except in Sheffield. Also, the proportion of people buying instant coffee was always higher than that of those purchasing fresh coffee in all the cities.

In London and Coventry, while the number of London's people who drank tea or coffee at a café was about 61%, the figure for Coventry was slightly higher, at around 64%. Meanwhile, roughly 48% of citizens in Coventry had a habit of buying instant coffee, which was around 3% higher than London's residents. The proportions of those purchasing fresh coffee in these two cities were similar, at around 44% and 43% respectively.

As for the other two cities, having coffee or tea at a café made up the highest percentage of people in Oxford (62%), followed by Wales and Sheffield, at approximately 54% and 39% respectively. Also, around 53% of people in Wales and Oxford chose to buy instant coffee, compared to 50% of those in Sheffield. Finally, the percentages of people buying fresh coffee in Wales and Sheffield witnessed a close similarity, at around 35%, while Oxford's number was slightly higher, at roughly 38%. (231 words)

Day 1　Line graph

(Writing Task 1)

You should spend about 20 minutes on this task.

> *The graph below shows the number of tourists visiting Brighton, the UK between 2009 and 2016.*
>
> *Summarise the information by selecting and reporting the main features and make comparisons where relevant.*

Write at least 150 words.

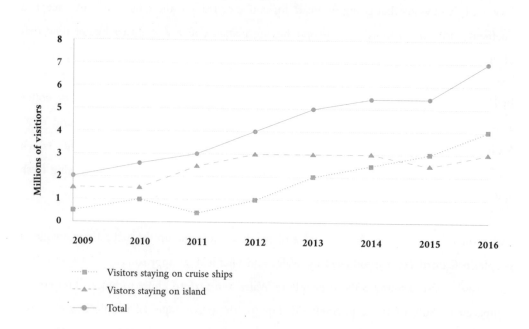

Number of tourists visiting Brighton, UK (2009-2016)

四段文章

第一段	第二段	第三段	第四段
改寫題目	整體趨勢	重要細節	重要細節

高分範文

The line graph illustrates how many visitors traveled to Brighton, the UK over a 7-year period from 2009 to 2016.

Overall, the total numbers of tourists visiting Brighton, the UK increased during the whole period. Additionally, the figure for visitors staying on cruise ships was lower than that for those choosing to stay on the island during most of the period.

In 2009, the total number of tourists who traveled to Brighton, the UK stood at 2 million, 1.5 million of whom chose for staying on the island, whereas the rest decided to stay on cruise ships. Over the following two years, the number of visitors staying on cruise ships significantly dropped, reaching its bottom of just under 0.5 million, but that of those staying on the island was more popular, with 2.5 million visitors.

In the final year (2016), Brighton, the UK witnessed a sharp rise to 7 million in the total number of visitors. Similarly, the number of tourists staying on cruise ships experienced a sharp increase to 4 million, surpassing that of those staying on the island (3 million). (182 words)

Day 2　Table

(Writing Task 1)

You should spend about 20 minutes on this task.

> *The tables below give information about sales of Fairtrade*-labelled fabric and apples in 2010 and 2015 in five European countries.*
>
> *Summarise the information by selecting and reporting the main features and make comparisons where relevant.*

Write at least 150 words.

Sales of Fairtrade-labelled tea and apples (2010-2015)

Fabric	2010 (millions of euros)	2015 (millions of euros)
France	1.5	20
Switzerland	3	6
Denmark	1.8	2
Italy	1	1.7
Germany	0.8	1

Apples	2010 (millions of euros)	2015 (millions of euros)
France	15	47
Switzerland	1	5.5
Denmark	0.6	4
Italy	1.8	1
Germany	2	0.9

*Fairtrade: a category of products for which farmers from developing countries have been paid an officially agreed fair price

四段文章

第一段	第二段	第三段	第四段
改寫題目	整體趨勢	重要細節	重要細節

高分範文

The two tables illustrate the figure of money spent on Fairtrade fabric and apples in two different years (2010 and 2015) in France, Switzerland, Denmark, Italy and Germany.

Overall, it is apparent that France saw the highest levels of expenditure on the two products. Also, sales of Fairtrade fabric ascended in all five European countries from 2010 to 2015, but those of Fairtrade apples went up in three out of the five countries.

In 1999, Switzerland had the highest sales of Fairtrade fabric, at €3 million, while revenue from Fairtrade apples was highest in France, at €15 million. In 2015, however, sales of Fairtrade fabric in France rose to €20 million, and this was over three times higher than those of Switzerland's for Fairtrade fabric. The year 2015 also saw dramatic increases in the money spent on Fairtrade apples in France and Switzerland by €32 million and €4.5 million respectively.

Sales of the two Fairtrade products were much lower in Denmark, Italy and Germany. In both years, sales of Fairtrade fabric slightly increased and revenue remained at €2 million or below in all three countries. Finally, it is noticeable that expenses spent on Fairtrade apples descended in Italy and Germany from 1.8 to 1 and 2 to 0.9 million respectively. (210 words)

Day 2   Pie chart

(Writing Task 1)

You should spend about 20 minutes on this task.

> *The charts below show the average percentages in typical meals of three types of nutrients, all of which may be unhealthy if eaten too much.*
>
> *Summarise the information by selecting and reporting the main features and make comparisons where relevant.*

Write at least 150 words.

Average percentages of MSG, trans fat, and artificial sweeteners in typical meals consumed in the UK

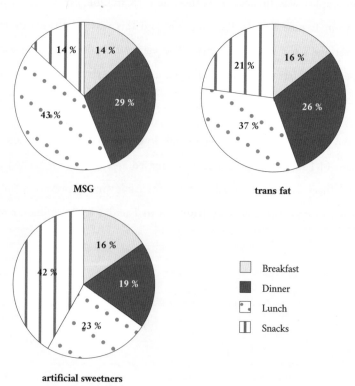

MSG

trans fat

artificial sweetners

Breakfast
Dinner
Lunch
Snacks

四段文章

第一段	第二段	第三段	第四段
改寫題目	整體趨勢	重要細節	重要細節

高分範文

The three pies show how much MSG, trans fat and artificial sweeteners are consumed in the three different meals in the UK, and they are detrimental for health if consumed plenty in quantity.

Overall, it is obvious that the majority of MSG and trans fat are consumed at dinner, while the maximum quantity of artificial sweeteners is eaten in snacks. In contrast, breakfast has the lowest percentages for all three additives.

Dinner and lunch have large proportions for both MSG (43% for dinner and 29% for lunch) and trans fat (37% for dinner and 26% for lunch). However, the figures of artificial sweeteners consumed at dinner and lunch are much lower at 23% and 19% respectively.

In terms of breakfast and snacks, both account for 14% MSG. For trans fat, snacks occupy 21%, and breakfast is slightly lower at 16%. In terms of artificial sweeteners, although 42% of snacks are not natural, only 16% of breakfasts are made up from them. (161 Words)

Day 3   Map

(Writing Task 1)

You should spend about 20 minutes on this task.

The plans below show a public park when it first opened in 1950 and the same park today.

Summarise the information by selecting and reporting the main features and make comparisons where relevant.

Write at least 150 words.

(四段文章)

第一段	第二段	第三段	第四段
改寫題目	整體趨勢	重要細節	重要細節

Da'an Forest Park (1950)
5th Avenue

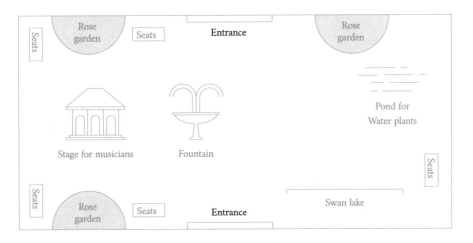

Da'an Forest Park (today)
5th Avenue

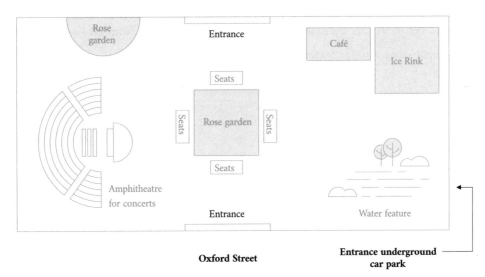

Oxford Street

**Entrance underground
car park**

The two maps show how Da'an Forest Park has been transformed from the opening in 1950 to the present.

Overall, Da'an Forest Park has been significantly changed after the constructions of several entertainment amenities over the period given.

In 1950, visitors could enter the park from the Northern or Southern entrance along 5th avenue or on Oxford street, but now they can get access to a new entrance from the underground car park. A fountain was located at the center of the park and a large stage for musicians was situated on the left-hand side of the fountain, but now both are superseded by a huge, square-shaped rose garden enclosed by many seats and by a large, circular area: an amphitheater for concerts.

In addition, in 1950, there was another rose garden to the east of the Northern entry, but it has been converted into a café. Also, a pond for water plants on the top right-hand corner has been renovated to make room for an ice rink, and a swan lake on the bottom has been replaced by a water feature. (182 words)

Day 3　Flow chart

You should spend about 20 minutes on this task.

> *The diagram below shows how ramen is manufactured.*
>
> *Summarise the information by selecting and reporting the main features and make comparisons where relevant.*

Write at least 150 words.

四段文章

第一段	第二段	第三段	第四段
改寫題目	整體趨勢	重要細節	重要細節

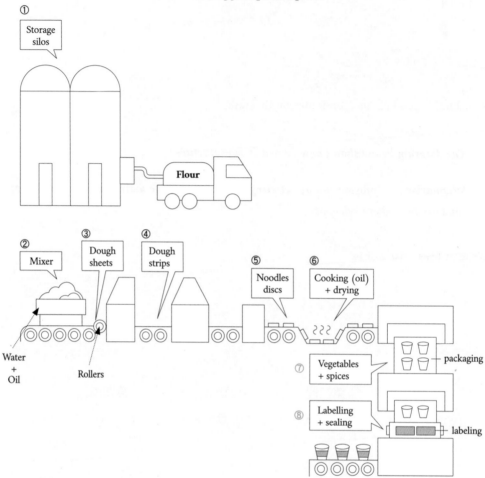

Manufacturing Jannpanese pasta

① Storage silos

Flour

② Mixer

Water + Oil

③ Dough sheets

Rollers

④ Dough strips

⑤ Noodles discs

⑥ Cooking (oil) + drying

⑦ Vegetables + spices

packaging

⑧ Labelling + sealing

labeling

The diagram shows the process of manufacturing Japanese ramen. Overall, the process consists of eight phases, from the storage of the flour in storage silos to the labelling of the final product.

At the beginning, the flour delivered is stored in the silos and then is pumped into a mixer by a truck. Water and oil are added to the flour and all the raw ingredients are mixed together. After all the ingredients are thoroughly mixed, rollers are used to make sheets of dough. Once dough strips are formed, they are molded by a machine to create ramen discs.

Next, these ramen discs are then cooked with oil and then left to dry. Once these ramen discs are dry, they are packed. In addition to the dried ramen, vegetables and spices are added to the packages. These pasta packages pass through the label machine, where they are sealed and labeled. This finalizes the process and they are ready to ship. (160 words)

心得筆記

2.5

一般組：書信解說

A. 書信的格式

雅思書信寫作主要測驗三個層面：**書信的寫作格式、書信的類型和書信的常用語**。雅思考試中心自 2006 年起已經明確規定考生不需要寫日期和地址。因此，雅思書信的寫作主要分三個部分：**稱呼、主體和署名**。

a. 稱呼

稱呼（salutation）有三種常用的方法：

(1) 如果收信人是企業、團體或機構，或不知道收信人的名字和性別時，就用 **Dear Sir or Madam** 或 **To whom it may concern**。

(2) 如果收信人是一個認識的人，但是這個人並不是熟悉或親密的朋友，那麼一般用 Dear Mr. (or Ms.) ＋ 收信人的姓，例如 **Dear Mr. Gates**、**Dear Ms. Clark**。

(3) 如果收信人是熟識的朋友，那麼一般用 **Dear ＋ 收信人的名**，例如 **Dear Jack**。

b. 主體部分

主體是根據信件的功能而變化。信件有不同的功能和目的，可以分為 8 種：

(1) 投訴信	(2) 詢問信	(3) 建議信	(4) 求助信
(5) 道歉信	(6) 感謝信	(7) 邀請信	(8) 求職

因為功能的不同，信件所使用的**語氣**和**用字**也不一樣。舉例來説，**投訴信**可以使用比較強烈的語氣外，其他信件則最好採用比較**禮貌**和**客氣**的用語。

另外，**收信人和你的關係**也需要考慮在內。如果和收信人比較熟悉，那麼就可以使用**非正式的語言**；相反地，如果和收信人不是非常熟悉，那麼用**正式的語言**比較恰當。例如寫信給很親密的朋友，信件的第一段甚至可以使用 How are you 這種比較口語化的句子，可以凸顯出與其親密或熟悉程度。

c. 信末的禮貌語和署名

信末常用 **yours sincerely, yours faithfully, yours truly, best regards**，這是最常見的用語；如果寫給很好的朋友，一般用 **yours, with love and best wishes, lots of love, many thanks** 等。簽名可以隨便寫，不一定要寫自己的真名，如 Mary, Jill, Billy, Tommy 等。

B. 書信的分類

a. 投訴信（letter of complaint）

投訴信是雅思作文中最常見的信件形式，出現的機會約 30%。

注意以下內容：

(1) 指出問題發生的前後文，譬如說，人物、時間、地點和原因。

(2) 說明問題所產生的後果。

(3) 提出支持自己一個特定的要求。

(4) 說明讀信的人可以做什麼來補救目前的局面。

(5) 建議解決方法並指出解決的時間限制。

(6) 不一定要使用激烈的言辭，最好使用比較禮貌的用語。

b. 諮詢信（inquiry letter）

諮詢信（和求助信）在雅思作文中也非常常見，出現的機會大概有 25%。

注意以下內容：

(1) 指明你所需要詢問的內容。

(2) 指出你為什麼需要這些內容。

(3) 指明你什麼時候需要內容。

(4) 避免語意含糊不清。

(5) 要求對方迅速回覆的時候要禮貌。

c. 求助信（request letter）

求助信和諮詢信其實其實很類似，區別在於求助信的**語氣更加懇切**。在寫求助信的時候，要注意以下內容：

(1) 詳述你所需要的幫助。

(2) 支持你自己的要求。

(3) 說服讀信的人答覆並且同意你的要求。

(4) 提出如何答謝對方，譬如說金錢。

(5) 說明時間期限。

d. 道歉信（letter of apology）

道歉信也是雅思作文的常考信件形式，出現的機會大概在 25% 左右。
注意以下內容：

(1) 對錯誤提出解釋，並且提出有說服力的觀點。

(2) 提出具體的解決方法。

(3) 考慮收信人的情緒。

(4) 建立信用和信任。

(5) 避免歸咎其他人。

(6) 用詞和語氣要禮貌體貼。

e. 建議信／提供訊息信

建議信在雅思考試中也比較普遍，出現的機會大概是 20%。建議信常常是收到對方
來信之後的一個回覆。在信件的開始部分，常出現 I am pleased to learn that... 或者
in/with reference to... 這些字眼，表示已經知道對方的計劃和意向。
在寫建議信的時候，要注意以下內容：

(1) 詳細提供具體的建議。

(2) 把最重要的建議放在最前面。

(3) 根據要求提供訊息。

(4) 強調所有重要的事項。

(5) 表達自己願意提供進一步的幫助。

f. 感謝信（letter of thanks）

感謝信在雅思作文中非常少見。即便出現，也經常是和其他的信件結合，譬如說道
歉信或者求助信。
在寫感謝信的時候，要注意以下內容：

(1) 由衷表示謝意。

(2) 強調所獲得支持的重要性。

(3) 維持和收信人的關係。

g. 邀請信（invitation letter）

邀請信在雅思作文中出現的機會也很低。

注意以下內容：

(1) 描述活動或計劃的內容。

(2) 指定日期、地址和時間。

(3) 指定被邀請參加的人。

(4) 如果恰當的話，清楚地說明著裝要求。

(5) 設定要求對方回信的日期。

h. 求職信（letter of application）

理論上，求職信應該是雅思作文的考題重點，因為移民之後，最重要的事情就是找工作。但是，在雅思考試中，求職信出現的機率卻很低。

在寫求職信的時候，要注意以下內容：

(1) 明確指出自己為什麼對該工作感興趣

(2) 信件內容要符合工作的要求。

(3) 具體回應僱主的要求，譬如說教育背景、工作經驗和個人才能。

(4) 留下地址和名字。

(5) 爭取做到簡潔和清晰，在信中突顯出個人工作方面的特色。

CHAPTER

3

你不知道的加分祕密：
詞語搭配（Collocation）

3.1

詞語搭配類型
你不知道的加分祕密：詞語搭配
（Collocation）

「詞語搭配」是一般英語學習者的最大問題。詞語搭配，英文翻譯是 collocation，col- 是一起，location 是位置，加起來就是「放在一起」。有些字天生就是和另外一些字注定要放在一起的。不僅僅是英文，中文也是這樣，例如我們說「**一件**事」，不說「一個事」；「**講**電話」，不說「談電話」。這就是「詞語搭配」。

詞語搭配用得好會讓語言變道地與流暢。我們講母語不會有問題，但當使用英文時，就常會「搭錯」詞。像中文的「開支票」，英文不是 open a check，而是 **write a check**；中文的「濃茶」，英文不是 heavy tea 也不是 thick tea，而是 **strong tea**。這種約定成俗的表達，很容易受到母語的影響直接翻譯而用錯，**因此在閱讀的時候，就要養成習慣，看得到誰應該跟誰「搭配」在一起，不能隨便亂點鴛鴦譜。**

為何要特別獨立出一個章節來探討詞語搭配呢？因為在雅思寫作中（甚至是雅思口說），使用正確或高級的詞語搭配會有加分作用，尤其是在 Lexical resource 這項評分標準。我們來看看以下證據，是考官根據劍橋雅思 15，Test 1 文章的評語。特別注意粗體字那句話，證明了詞語搭配的確會被考官注意到。

"The range of vocabulary is appropriate, with examples of less common items [long after / for / house / housing marekt] and **good use of collocations [claim ownership / a major headache / pay mortgage / natural disaster / The bottom line]**."

常見的詞語搭配有很多種，老師在這本書會舉出常見且會加分的 4 種類型：

1. Verb + Noun

2. Adj + Noun

3. Adv + Verb

4. Adv + Adj

(1) Verb + Noun

你知道「噴」香水，不是用 spread perfume，而是 **"wear"** perfume 嗎？

你知道「開」戰，不是用 open war，而是 **"wage"** war 嗎？

我們來測試一下你的詞語搭配能力。每一題 5 秒內想不到，那就表示你永遠想不到了。Are you ready? Go!

1. 放風箏　　：_____ a kite

2. 拼拼圖　　：_____ a jigsaw puzzle

3. 招來危險　：_____ danger

4. 補充能量　：_____ energy

5. 開始行動　：_____ an action

6. 培養好習慣：_____ good habits

已經過了一分鐘了。你想到幾個呢？看看老師的解答！

1. 放風箏　　　：**fly** a kite

2. 拼拼圖　　　：**do** a jigsaw puzzle

3. 招來危險　　：**invite** danger

4. 補充能量　　：**replenish** energy

5. 開始行動　　：**initiate** an action

6. 培養好習慣　：**cultivate** good habits

((2) Adj + Noun)

你知道「老」客戶不是 old customers，而是「**regular**」 customers 嗎？

每當你想要表達「漂亮的」風景，你只會寫／説：beautiful scenery 嗎？

其實也可以換成：

breathtaking, fantastic, impressive, magnificent, spectacular, stunning

+ scenery

((3) Adv + Verb)

例句 1：我「**非常**」喜歡你。

你只會寫下面這樣的搭配嗎？

→ I **very** like you.（此句文法有錯誤）

說明：very 雖然是副詞，但是只能拿來修飾形容詞，不能修飾動詞。

你知道可以用 really / enormously 來修飾 like 嗎？

→ I **really** like you. = I like you **a lot** / **enormously**.

例句 2：網路改變我們的生活**很大**。

你只會寫下面這樣的搭配嗎？

→ The Internet has changed our life **a lot**.

說明：你知道可以用 considerably / significantly / radically / dramatically 嗎？

原句變成了：

→ The Internet has changed our life **considerably** / **significantly** / **radically** / **dramatically**.

換一個不一樣的「副詞」來修飾動詞

不覺得讓整句話變高級多了嗎 ?!!!

甚至可以「移動副詞」，變成：

→ The Internet has radically changed our life.

說明：這樣的寫法讓修辭更漂亮，因為很清楚看到 radically 是修飾 changed。

(4) Adv + Adj

想表達「**相當**不一樣」，你只會寫 very different 嗎？

我們可以用 markedly / radically / significantly / strikingly / completely / entirely / quite / totally different。

想表達「**相當**不開心的」，你只會寫 very unhappy 嗎？

我們可以用 desperately / distinctly / dreadfully / terribly / wretchedly unhappy。

學生使用英文詞語搭配詞錯誤可能有 大主要原因：

1. 受到母語的干擾

主要是因為學生的母語使用直接轉移到英文，卻沒發覺這是錯誤的， 如，中文說的「**學習**知識」，很多學生就會寫成 learn knowledge 或 study knowledge，但是英文的 learn 和 study 是不會與 knowledge 搭配在一起，意義比較接近的英文搭配是 **gain** 或 **acquire** knowledge。「寫功課」**do** homework 不能寫成 write homework；「作研究」**do** research，也不能用 make research。**這些錯誤大多是學習者母語的干擾。**

2. 英文使用的過度類化

這一類型學習者的英文已經有一定的程度，但是常常只是把單字的中文語意背下來而已，卻不知其真正的意思，也就是當初背單字時少了查英英字典的習慣，因此沒有真正了解單字的用法，而產生了錯誤的搭配。 如，學生知道 **commit** crime （犯罪），但是表達「犯錯」時，卻不能寫 commit mistakes。想要表達「**犯錯**」時，應該用 **make** mistakes。我們來看看劍橋字典上面的英英解釋：

commit: to do something illegal or something that is considered wrong

E.g. to **commit** a crime / an offence / murder / fraud / robbery

 老師提醒

這些**詞語搭配**對於考試、書信撰寫都非常非常的重要，尤其是對於雅思來說更是，因為雅思寫作的評分標準之一就是看 **lexical resource**，也就是看單字的變化以及精準度。所謂的精準度就是用字是否道地與否，寫出正確的詞語搭配就是寫出精準的單字用法。**因此，想要考試得到高分，詞語搭配是不可或缺的。**

3.2

從牛津字典中學習詞語搭配

我們已經了解到詞語搭配的類型與其重要性了，但是我們該如何想出正確的詞語搭配呢？答案是，很難。即使有想到某些單字，但不代表它可以跟某些單字擺放在一起。我們來測試一下。

1. **對抗／減輕**疲勞　　→ _____ fatigue
2. **施加**處罰　　　　　→ _____ a penalty
3. **抑制**肺炎　　　　　→ _____ covid-19
4. **沖洗**照片　　　　　→ _____ a film
5. **扼殺**小孩的創意　　→ _____ children's creativity
6. **老**客戶　　　　　　→ _____ customers

你有想到答案了嗎？

1. **對抗／減輕**疲勞　　→　**eliminate** fatigue
2. **施加**處罰　　　　　→　**add** a penalty
3. **抑制**肺炎　　　　　→　**control** covid-19
4. **沖洗**照片　　　　　→　**wash** a film
5. **扼殺**小孩的創意　　→　**kill** children's creativity
6. **老**客戶　　　　　　→　**old** customers

以上也是你想到的答案嗎？恭喜你，只有答對一題，第三題是對的，其餘都是錯的。這就是我上述提到的問題，**即使你有想到某些單字，但不代表它可以跟某些單字擺放在一起**。正確答案如下：

1. **對抗／減輕**疲勞   →   **combat / fight off / reduce** fatigue

2. **施加**處罰   →   **impose** a penalty

3. **抑制**肺炎   →   **control / contain** covid-19

4. **沖洗**照片   →   **develop** a film

5. **扼殺**小孩的創意   →   **stifle** children's creativity

6. **老**客戶   →   **regular** customers

你有發現嗎？是不是很多單字都背過，但是卻不知道原來它們可以這樣組合在一起。沒關係，老師教你一個簡單、快速，最重要的是，正確的方法，保證你找到之後的答案一定是 100% 正確的。

老師介紹你一個超讚的工具：牛津詞語搭配字典（Online OXFORD Collocation Dictionary）。它也有網路版，而且是免費的！

注意：**在使用字典輸入你想要的字詞時，要注意大小寫，可能會因為開頭大寫而搜尋不到。**

接下來老師教你如何使用這本超棒祕笈。我們以上述提到的例子來解釋：

1. **對抗／減輕**疲勞   →   _____ fatigue

2. **施加**處罰   →   _____ a penalty

3. **抑制**肺炎   →   _____ covid-19

4. **沖洗**照片   →   _____ a film

5. **扼殺**小孩的創意   →   _____ children's creativity

6. **老**客戶   →   _____ customers

以 (1) **消除**疲勞來說明，此時我們想要的單字是**消除**，但是腦海中就是不知道哪一個單字才是正確的單字，如果知道疲勞時 fatigue 的話，就可以解決這個問題了。參照以下步驟：

1. 用 fatigue 查詢**牛津詞語搭配**這本字典。
2. 再找到 **verb + fatigue** 這裡面有 suffer from, drop (down) with / combat, fight (off), reduce 這兩組單字。
3. 再從這兩組單字中，尋找**你認識的單字**以及跟你所想語意近似的字。
4. 這兩組字中，跟**對抗／減輕**比較接近的是 **combat, fight (off), reduce** 這組字。

fatigue noun	
great tiredness 疲勞	
ADJ. + fatigue	extreme, severe | growing | mental, physical
Verb + fatigue	suffer from, drop (down) with | combat, fight (off), reduce

因此，**對抗／減輕疲勞**的英文是：**combat, fight (off), reduce fatigue**。以後用同樣的方式，就可以找到你想要的單字，也能組合出正確的單字搭配。

✏️ **心得筆記**

3-3

從雅思閱讀中學習詞語搭配

學習詞語搭配除了用詞語搭配字典之外，還有另外一個更好的方式，就是從閱讀中學習正確且高級的詞語搭配，而且最好直接從雅思閱讀的文章中學習最好，因為這樣就可以一石二鳥，一邊準備**雅思閱讀**，同時也一起準備**雅思寫作**，甚至可以運用在**雅思口說**中，就變成一石三鳥了。

如何在雅思閱讀中學習詞語搭配呢？首先，要先了解常見的詞語搭配類型，如下：

1. **Verb+ Noun** （動詞　+　名詞）
2. **Adj　+ Noun** （形容詞 +　名詞）
3. **Adv + Verb** （副詞　　+　動詞）
4. **Adv + Adj** （副詞　　+　形容詞）

如果在文章中看到這樣的組合，就是漂亮的詞語搭配。

我們來看看下面這篇（非雅思閱讀的）範例：

I [1]**experienced a roller coaster of emotions** when my daughter was born (many different emotions one after another). During my wife's pregnancy, I [2]**was ridiculously excited about** the prospect of becoming a dad. On the big day, I'd imagined that everything would go smoothly and we'd [3]**be blissfully happy** – but there were complications during the delivery and my wife had to have emergency surgery while I waited in the reception area, [4]**worried sick** (very worried).

My wife [5]**was visibly disappointed** (it was obvious that she was disappointed) that I wasn't by her side when she woke up from surgery. She didn't say anything – she's not really one to [6]**show her feelings**; she prefers to [7]**bottle up her emotions** (keep her emotions hidden inside her) – but I knew I had let her down and I [8]**was terribly sorry** that I had [9]**lost my temper** (lost control and shown anger).

翻譯

我女兒出生時，我的 [1] **心情忐忑不安**。我老婆懷孕期間，我 [2] **相當興奮**要當老爸了。我想像那一天每件事情都會很順利，而且我們也會 [3] **非常開心**，但是生產過程中出現一些併發症，所以我老婆必須緊急手術。我在手術房外面 [4] **相當著急**地等待著。

我老婆 [5] **看起來非常失望**，因為她手術後醒來時，我沒有在她身邊。她沒有說什麼。她屬於不擅長 [6] **表達情緒**的人；她比較喜歡 [7] **隱藏情緒**，但我知道我讓她失望了，而我也 [8] **相當抱歉**，因為我 [9] **發脾氣了**。

詞語搭配

1. | **Verb + Noun** | experience a roller coaster of emotions　心情忐忑
= feel a roller coaster of emotions

2. | **Adv + Adj** | be ridiculously excited about...　對……感到非常興奮
= be extremely excited about
= be highly excited about
= be terribly excited about
= be tremendously excited about

3. | **Adv + Adj** | be blissfully happy　非常開心
= be amazingly happy
= be surprisingly happy
= be radiantly happy

4. | **Adv + Adj** | be worried sick　非常擔心
= be extremely worried
= be terribly worried
= be desperately worried

5. **Adv + Adj** be visibly disappointed （表情）顯露失望

= be bitterly upset

= be deeply frustrated

= be desperately saddened

= be terribly disgruntled

= be extremely discontented

6. **Verb + Noun** show one's feelings 表現出情緒

= express one's feelings

= release one's feelings

= give vent to one's feelings

= vent one's feelings

7. **Verb + Noun** bottle up one's emotions 壓抑心情

= hide one's emotions

= stifle one's emotions

= suppress one's emotions

8. **Adv + Adj** be terribly sorry 非常抱歉

= be awfully sorry

= be deeply sorry

= be genuinely sorry

= be truly sorry

9. **Verb + Noun** lost one's temper 發脾氣

= fly into one's temper

= fly into a rage

看完上述的示範，應該比較清楚如何從閱讀中尋找詞語搭配了嗎？接下來我們來看一篇雅思閱讀的考古題，藉由雅思閱讀來提升雅思寫作與口說的評分標準之一：**Lexical resource**。

[1]MAKING THE MOST OF TRENDS

Experts from Harvard Business School give advice to managers

Most managers can identify the major trends of the day. However, during the course of [2]**conducting research** in a number of industries and cooperating directly with companies, we have found that managers often fail to recognize the less obvious but [3]**profound ways** these trends are influencing consumers' aspirations, attitudes, and behaviours. This is especially true of trends that managers view as peripheral to their [4]**core markets**.

詞語搭配

1. **Verb + Noun** make the most of... 充分利用……

= capitalize on trends

= take advantage of trends

2. **Verb + Noun** conduct research 做研究

= do research

= carry out research

= undertake research

3. **Adj + Noun** profound ways 深入的方式

= insightful ways

= deep ways

4. **Adj + Noun** core markets 核心市場

Many overlook trends in their innovation strategies, adopt a wait-and-see approach, and unfortunately let competitors [5]**take the lead**. At a minimum, such responses mean missed profit opportunities. At the extreme, they can [6]**jeopardize a company** by [7]**ceding to** rivals the opportunity to [8]**transform the industry**. The are two purposes in this article: to [9]**spur managers** to think more expansively about how trends could [10]**engender new value propositions** in their core markets and to provide some [11]**high-level advice** on how to make market research and product development personnel more proficient at analyzing and exploiting trends.

詞語搭配

5. **Verb + Noun** take the lead　帶頭、領先

6. **Verb + Noun** jeopardize a company　危害公司
= endanger a company
= put a company in danger
= imperil a company
= hazard a company
= threaten a company

7. **Verb + Noun** cede the opportunity　放棄機會
= cede the opportunity to rivals
= yield the opportunity
= concede the opportunity
= relinquish the opportunity

8. **Verb + Noun** transform the industry　革新產業
= reform the industry
= revolutionize the industry
= change the industry
= modernize the industry

9. **Verb + Noun** spur managers　鼓勵經理
= urge managers
= encourage managers

- = prompt managers
- = impel managers
- = stimulate managers
- = inspire managers

10. **Verb + Noun** engender new value propositions　產生新的價值主張
- = produce new value propositions
- = create new value propositions
- = generate new value propositions

11. **Adj + Noun** high-level advice　高層次的建議
- = sophisticated advice
- = advanced advice

One strategy, known as 'infuse and augment', is to design a product or service that [12]**retains most of the attributes and functions** of existing products but adds others that [13]**address the needs and desires** caused by a major trend. A case in point in the Poppy range of handbags, which the firm Coach created in response to the [14]**economic downturn** of 2008. The Coach brand had been a symbol of opulence and luxury for nearly 70 years. The most obvious reaction to the downturn would have been to lower prices, but that would have risked [15]**cheapening the brand's image**. Instead, they [16]**initiated a consumer-research project** revealing that customers were eager to [17]**lift themselves and the country out of tough times**. Adopting these insights, Coach [18]**launched the lower-priced Poppy handbags**, which were in vibrant colors, and looked more youthful and playful than conventional Coach products. Creating the sub-brand helped Coach [19]**avert an across-the-board price cut**. In contrast to the many companies that responded to the recession by [20]**cutting prices**, Coach regarded the new consumer mindset as an opportunity for innovation.

12. Verb + Noun retain most of the attributes and functions　保有大部分特色功能
= keep most of the attributes and functions
= maintain most of the attributes and functions
= preserve most of the attributes and functions

13. Verb + Noun address the needs and desires　滿足需求與渴望
= fulfill the needs and desires
= meet the needs and desires
= satisfy the needs and desires
= live up to the needs and desires

14. Adj + Noun economic downturn　經濟不景氣／蕭條／衰退
= economic decline
= economic slump
= recession
= depression

15. Verb + Noun cheapen the brand's image　貶低品牌形象
= belittle the brand's image
= demean the brand's image
= lower the brand's image
= degrade the brand's image
= denigrate the brand's image

16. Verb + Noun initiate a consumer-research project　開始了消費者研究計畫
= start a consumer-research project
= begin a consumer-research project
= launch a consumer-research project
= commence a consumer-research project

17. **Verb + Noun** lift oneself and the country out of tough times
拯救自己和國家免於艱苦歲月

18. **Verb + Noun** launch the lower-priced Poppy handbags   發行低價的 Poppy 包
= unveil the lower-priced Poppy handbags
= unleash the lower-priced Poppy handbags
= introduce the lower-priced Poppy handbags

19. **Verb + Adj + Noun** avert an across-the-board price cut   避免全面的降價
= avoid a sweeping price cut
= prevent a universal price cut
= deter a wide-ranging price cut
= stop an across-the-board price cut
= ward off an across-the-board price cut

20. **Verb + Noun** cut prices   降價
= reduce prices
= slash prices
= push down prices
= bring down prices
= mark down prices

 老師提醒

考生如果能夠抓到此章節的閱讀方式，就能達到魚與熊掌都能兼得的效果，因為一邊準備雅思閱讀的過程中，還可以順便準備雅思寫作與口説，真的是一舉數得啊！

CHAPTER

4

Task 2 學術寫作

4.1

題目類型分類

雅思寫作的問句方式很多元,如果沒有清楚「回答題目」,是會被嚴重扣分。因此,
了解如何寫出高分文章之前,先來了解雅思常見的問句方式,總共有 5 種:

1. **To what extent do you agree or disagree**
2. **Discuss both views and give your opinion**
3. **Advantages and disadvantages**
4. **Causes and solutions**
5. **Two-part questions**

> ### 1. To what extent do you agree or disagree

Rich countries often give financial aid to poor countries, but it does not solve the poverty,
so rich countries should give other types of help to poor countries rather than financial aid.
To what extent do you agree or disagree?

針對這種題目,有兩種文章結構建議考生使用:

Structure 1 of Agree/Disagree essays

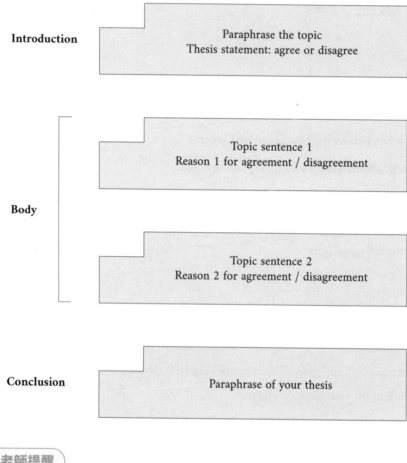

Introduction
> Paraphrase the topic
> Thesis statement: agree or disagree

Body
> Topic sentence 1
> Reason 1 for agreement / disagreement

> Topic sentence 2
> Reason 2 for agreement / disagreement

Conclusion
> Paraphrase of your thesis

老師提醒

第一種就是在兩段的中間段落，都是解釋為何同意或不同意你自己的觀點，也就是說兩段的觀點是一樣的，只是提供兩個理由。

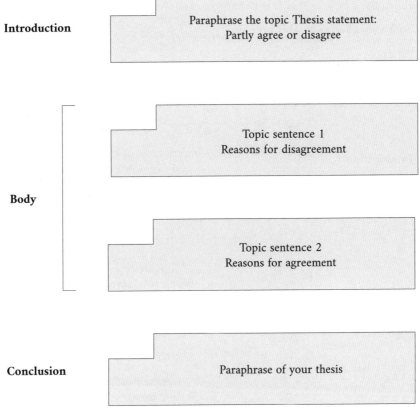

Introduction

Paraphrase the topic Thesis statement:
Partly agree or disagree

Body

Topic sentence 1
Reasons for disagreement

Topic sentence 2
Reasons for agreement

Conclusion

Paraphrase of your thesis

老師提醒

第二種就是在兩段的中間段落，分別解釋為何同意以及不同意你自己的觀點，也就是說，**第二段是讓步段，去承認反方論點的好。第三段才是你自己真正的論點。**這本書後面的文章，大部分是使用這個結構，因為論點會更加多元，也可以避免考生寫到重複的論點卻渾然不知。

2. Discuss both views and give your opinion

Some people believe that studying at university or college is the best route to a successful career, while others believe that it is better to get a job straight after school.
Discuss both views and give your opinion.

Structure of both-view essays

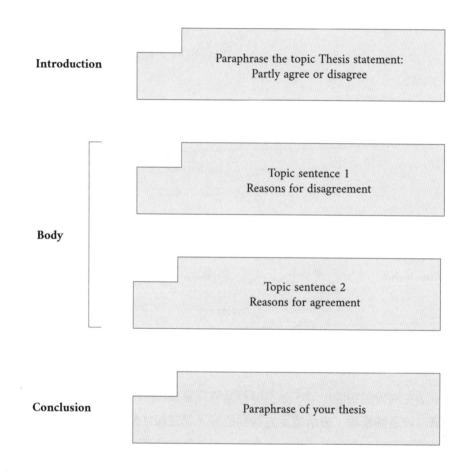

Introduction — Paraphrase the topic Thesis statement:
Partly agree or disagree

Body

Topic sentence 1
Reasons for disagreement

Topic sentence 2
Reasons for agreement

Conclusion — Paraphrase of your thesis

遇到這種題目時要特別注意，考題明確指出 Discuss both views and give your opinion 這句話，很多考生有看卻沒有真的看懂。題目要求考生要討論雙方觀點，並且指出你的立場。**尤其是前者，一定要記住雙方觀點都要討論到，千萬不能只有選邊站，這樣可是會被嚴重扣分的喔！**

換句話說，**建議考生第二段寫出讓步段，去承認反方論點的好。第三段才是你自己真正的論點**，就可以滿足題目要求了。

✏ 心得筆記

3. Advantages and disadvantages

Public libraries will soon no longer be housed in a building as all facilities and books will be available online for all to access.

Discuss the advantages and disadvantages of public libraries only existing online.

Structure of advantage-and-disadvantage essays

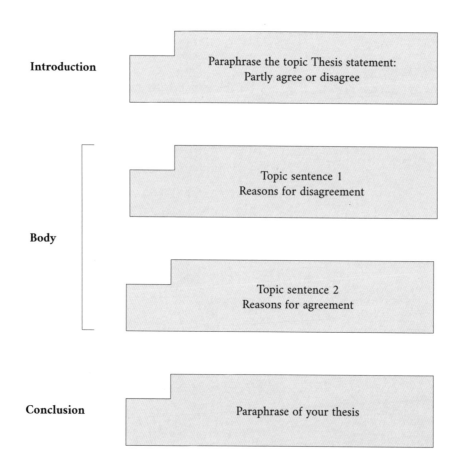

Introduction

Paraphrase the topic Thesis statement:
Partly agree or disagree

Body

Topic sentence 1
Reasons for disagreement

Topic sentence 2
Reasons for agreement

Conclusion

Paraphrase of your thesis

4. Discuss causes and/or solutions

In the developed world, average life expectancy is increasing. What problems will this cause for individuals and society? Suggest some measures that could be taken to reduce the impact of ageing populations.

Structure of cause/solution essays

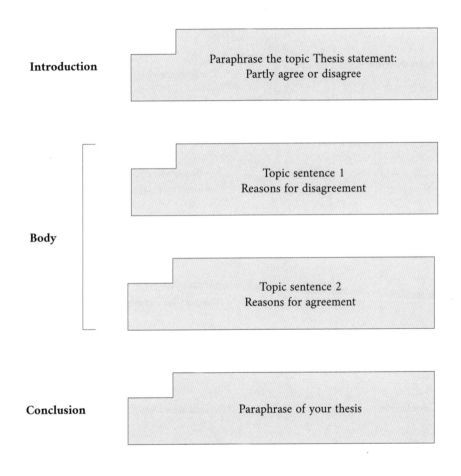

Introduction — Paraphrase the topic Thesis statement: Partly agree or disagree

Body — Topic sentence 1 Reasons for disagreement

Topic sentence 2 Reasons for agreement

Conclusion — Paraphrase of your thesis

5. Two-part questions

There are social, medical and technical problems associated with the use of mobile phones. What forms do they take? Do you agree that the problems outweigh the benefits of mobile phones?

Structure of two-part-question essays

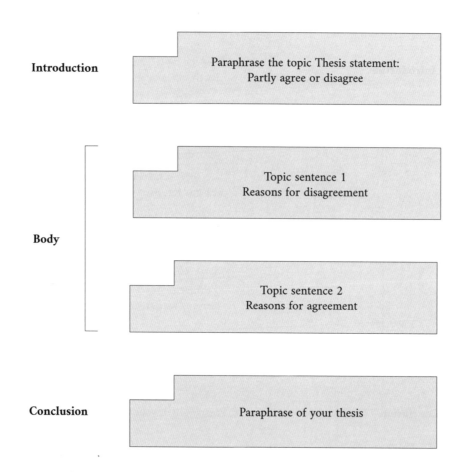

Introduction
Paraphrase the topic Thesis statement:
Partly agree or disagree

Body
Topic sentence 1
Reasons for disagreement

Topic sentence 2
Reasons for agreement

Conclusion
Paraphrase of your thesis

4.2

大綱式寫作

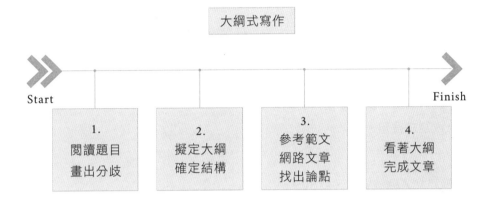

大綱式寫作是老師自創的招式，總共有 4 個步驟：

1. 閱讀題目，劃出分歧

仔細閱讀完題目之後，找出題目的正反方，目的是為了下一步驟。最重要的是，在此就要決定你的立場，支持還是反對題目，或是選某一邊站。這個步驟看似簡單，但是也是最多同學失分的地方，因為常常在第一段時沒有很清楚地讓考官了解到你的立場是什麼。

例如：

Some people think that all university students should study whatever they **like**. Others believe that they should only be allowed to study subjects that will be **useful** in the future, such as those related to science and technology. Discuss both views and give your own opinion.

此時的分歧點就是 like 和 useful。注意，雖然找出分歧點了，但是一定要在主旨句清楚表達你的真正立場到底是 like 還是 useful，否則會嚴重扣分，因為考官會搞不清楚你整篇文章的立場，而在 Task Achievement 這個評分標準中扣分喔！

2. 擬定大綱，確定結構

找出正反方後，就可以擬定簡易版大綱，確定整篇文章的結構。
第一段　While...（**反方**），（**正方**）
第二段　反方論點。此段是**讓步段**。
第三段　正方論點。此段才是你的**真正立場**。
第四段　改寫主旨句。

3. 參考範文／網路文章，找出論點：

這個步驟就是最麻煩，也是這本書的精華。此步驟可利用文章題目關鍵字從網路上搜尋（非雅思）的文章，或從雅思高分範文中，萃取其中最相關也最重要的內容和單字，寫出完整版的大綱。**切記，這裡的內容只能是單字或片語，不能是完整的句子，否則就是抄襲。而且越多符號越好**，例如：（表示：因→果）、（果←因）或是 +（為 and）等。**更重要的是，大綱中也要想好文章的語意邏輯，最好要出現很多過渡詞（however, therefore, instead, despite, due to, in fact, on the other hand）或從屬連接詞（but, although, while, because, if, when）**。

以下為擬定大綱時，參考的符號使用：

符號表	
and	＋
or	／
not	✕
without	w/o

S + V ... because S + V ...	←
due to / owing to /as a result of	←
Because + S + V ..., S + V ...	→
If + S + V ..., S + V ...	→
Therefore/ Thus, S + V...	→
S + V ..., and therefor/thus + S + V ...	→
however, on the other hand, instead, On the contrary	↔
for example, for instance, a case in point	e.g.
同位語	=
That is,	=
In other words,	=
形容詞子句：who/which	()
rise / increase	↑
reduce / decrease	↓
平行結構 A, B, and C	（1）A （2）B （3）C
the government	gov't
more than	>

---

4. 看著大綱，完成文章

如果前三步驟都完成的話，第四步驟就是看著完整版的大綱，用自己學過的文法、句型清楚地寫出全文。

Introduction

Paraphrase the topic
Thesis statement: While 反方論點，正方論點

Body

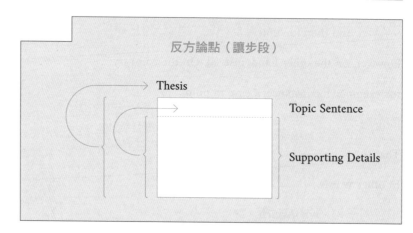

反方論點（讓步段）

Thesis

Topic Sentence

Supporting Details

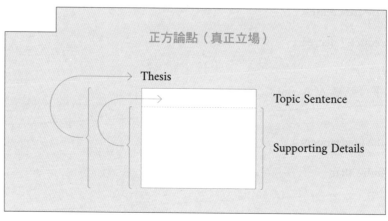

正方論點（真正立場）

Thesis

Topic Sentence

Supporting Details

Conclusion

Paraphrase of your thesis

示範題目

Some people think that all university students should study whatever they like. Others believe that they should only be allowed to study subjects that will be useful in the future, such as those related to science and technology.

Discuss both these views and give your own opinion.

大綱式寫作步驟解析

1. 閱讀題目，劃出分歧（破解題目）：

Some people think that all university students should study whatever they **like**. Others believe that they should only be allowed to study subjects that will be **useful** in the future...

* 分歧點： useful vs. like

2. 擬定大綱，確定結構：

第一段 : While **useful, like**.

第二段 : **useful**

第三段 : **like**

第四段 : paraphrase your thesis

3. 參考範文／網路文章，找出論點：

2nd paragraph	
Subject:	a useful major
Argument:	ensure job stability + contribute to the society
Supporting Ideas:	a. instrumental: ensure job stability + contribute to the society if X directly lead to a career path → X which path to take (1) end up feeling confused (2) the passion of a certain major fades away ⇔ information technology, engineering + medicine ← the most value for money + return on investment b. a focus on useful majors (1) new inventions (2) economic advance (3) growing future prosperity an increasing number (1) bridge the gap of any knowledge (2) skill in the economy

3rd paragraph	
Subject:	the major they like
Argument:	motivation + opportunities
Supporting Ideas:	a. if X like → X motivated + become experts of the chosen fields Though make a fortune, salary earned + job satisfaction X correlated ← $ X function as a motivator b. studying something they love → a window onto the world = more chances cast their net wide (1) find more opportunities (2) opportunities might even find them stories of passion go awry ← (1) losing focus (2) lacking zeal (3) settling for mediocre X, if students (1) stick sth you love (2) do your best (3) strive for excellence → transmute interest into their favorite job

4. 看著大綱，完成文章。

高分範文

People have [1]**divergent opinions** about whether students should choose the major they like or a useful one at university. While some argue that it would be better for students to major in useful subjects, I believe that everyone should be able to study the course they [2]**are deeply interested in**.

Admittedly, choosing a useful major will [3]**be instrumental for** students to ensure job stability and contribute to the society. [4]**From the perspective of** job stability, if students select a degree that doesn't directly lead to a career path, they will have difficulty trying to decide which path to take. They might end up [5]**feeling confused about** what to do next after [6]**the passion of a certain major fades away**. However, if students choose courses like information technology, engineering and medicine, these are more likely to be more beneficial than certain art majors because they give students the most value for money and [7]**return on investment**. [8]**On the society level**, a focus on useful majors, like technology in higher education, could [9]**bring about** new inventions, [10]**economic advance**, and [11]**growing future prosperity**. Besides, an increasing number of students who choose these subjects can [12]**bridge the gap of** any knowledge and skill in the economy.

In spite of these arguments, I believe that students should choose the major they like for two reasons: motivation and opportunities. First, if they choose a major they don't like, they cannot [13]**be truly motivated** and even become the experts of the chosen fields. Though they may [14]**make a fortune**, however, salary earned and job satisfaction [15]**is not highly correlated** because money cannot [16]**function as a motivator** in a happy workforce. Second, studying something they love gives them a window on the world, that is, more opportunities. If they cast their net wide, they will find more opportunities; sometimes, some opportunities might even find them. Of course, [17]**many stories of passions go awry** due to losing focus, lacking zeal, and settling for mediocre. However, if students [18]**stick with something** they really love, [19]**try their utmost**, and [20]**strive for excellence**, studying what they love may transmute interest into their favorite job.

In conclusion, only focusing on the useful subjects might appear sensible and helpful, but I still believe people have the right to study what they like in the current system. (382 words)

1. **Adj + Noun** divergent opinions　不同的意見
=　conflicting opinions
=　mixed opinions

2. **Adv + Adj** be deeply interested in...　對⋯⋯很有興趣
=　be intensely interested in
=　be keenly interested in
=　be particularly interested in
=　be passionately interested in
=　be greatly interested in
=　be genuinely interested in

3. **be + Adj + Preposition** be instrumental for　有幫助的
=　be helpful for
=　be beneficial for
=　be useful for
=　be advantageous for

4. **Preposition + Noun** from the perspective of　從⋯⋯角度
=　from the angle of
=　from the viewpoint of
=　from the standpoint of

5. **Verb + Adj + Preposition** feel confused about...　感到困惑
=　feel puzzled about
=　feel mystified by
=　feel feeling baffled by

6. **Noun + Verb** the passion of a certain major fades away　對某科系的熱情消逝

    = the passion of a certain major cools

    = the passion of a certain major wanes

7. **Noun + Preposition** return on investment　投資報酬

    = profits of investment

    = rewards of investment

    = yields of investment

    = revenues of investment

    = earnings of investment

    = proceedings of investment

8. **Preposition + Noun** on the society level　從社會的角度來看

    = from the perspective of the society

    = from the viewpoint of the society

    = from the standpoint of the society

    = from the angle of the society

9. **Verb + Noun** bring about new inventions　帶來新發明

    = cause new inventions

    = lead to new inventions

    = result in new inventions

    = trigger new inventions

    = give rise to new inventions

    = yield new inventions

10. **Adj + Noun** economic advance　經濟進步／成長

    = economic development

    = economic progress

    = economic growth

11. **Adj + Noun** growing future prosperity　前景看好

= increasing future prosperity

= rising future prosperity

12. **Verb + Noun** bridge the gap of...　補上……的缺口

= fill the gap of

= seal the gap of

13. **Adv + Adj** be truly motivated　真正被激發

= be highly motivated

= be strongly motivated

14. **Verb + Noun** make a fortune　賺大錢

= make a killing

= win a fortune

15. **Adv + Adj** be not highly correlated　非密切相關

= be not closely correlated

= be not strongly correlated

16. **Verb + Preposition + Noun** serve as a motivator　成為激發的動力

= function as a motivator

17. **Noun + Verb** many stories of passions go awry　許多有熱情的故事變調了

= many stories of passions go wrong

18. **Verb + Preposition + Noun** stick with something　堅持某件事

= persist with something

= persevere with something

= adhere to something

= insist on Ving something

注意：insist on 後面要加上 Ving，因為 on 是介系詞。

19. **Verb + Noun** try one's utmost   盡全力

= try one's best

= do one's utmost

= do one's damnedest

20. **Verb + Preposition + Noun** strive for excellence   盡善盡美

= endeavor for excellence

= make every effort for excellence

心得筆記

4.3

20 天搞定 Task 2（Day 4 – Day 23）

Task 2 常考的主題類型有 22 種，此章節訓練考生其中最常出現的 20 種。

Day 4　Education

The role of education is to prepare children for the modern world. Schools should cut art and music out of the curriculum so that children can focus on useful subjects such as information technology.

To what extent do you agree or disagrees with this statement?

大綱式寫作步驟解析

1. 閱讀題目，劃出分歧（破解題目）：

The role of education is to prepare children for the modern world. Schools should cut **art and music** out of the curriculum so that children can focus on useful subjects such as **information technology**.

* 分歧點：art + music vs. information technology (IT)

2. 擬定大綱，確定結構：

擬定大綱，確定結構

第一段：While **IT**, **art + music**.

第二段：**IT**

第三段：**art + music**

第四段：paraphrase your thesis

3. 參考範文／網路文章，找出論點：

2nd paragraph	
Subject:	information technology
Argument:	obtain hands-on experience + earn good money
Supporting Ideas:	a. are given practical studies X theoretical ones 　　= X are confined to books/ textbooks 　　← allocate large budget 　　← new information about computing + update their savvy b. high earning potential 　　← are highly prized in modern businesses 　　→ get a leg up on the competition with these handy, professional skills

| 3rd paragraph | |

3rd paragraph	
Subject:	art + music
Argument:	promote creativity + express feelings
Supporting Ideas:	a. w/o training of imaginative + creative thinking → struggle to grow into dynamic, critical individuals ⇔ if are gifted in their creative abilities (1) help them further nurture their talents (2) sharpen the cognitive skills e.g. when they join the workforce (1) feel more independent (2) boost their confidence (3) become bold in decision making b. w/o the linguistic capabilities to clearly express themselves + communicate successfully → convey meanings through pictures, symbols, + rhythm teachers utilize children's artworks → gain an insight into what they think + feel

4. 看著大綱，完成文章。

Many people think schools may [1]**face a dilemma of** whether they should replace art and music with information technology so as to [2]**equip** students **with** the ability to face the challenges in this modern world. While information technology is [3]**of paramount importance** for students, I believe subjects like art and music are also indispensable.

Admittedly, if students choose information technology (IT) courses, they can obtain hands-on experience and [4]**earn good money**. From the perspective of practical experience, IT students are given practical studies rather than theoretical ones. That is, scholars [5]**are** not **confined to** books or textbooks because most universities allocate large budget to add new information on computing and [6]**update their savvy** continuously. Moreover, undoubtedly, a pursuit of IT courses can result in high earning potential because IT courses are highly prized in modern businesses. Therefore, graduates can [7]**get a leg up on** others in the competition with these handy, professional skills.

Despite these arguments, I believe that art is an essential subject because students should learn to promote their creativity and express their emotions and feelings. First, without the training of imaginative and creative thinking, students will struggle to grow into dynamic, critical individuals when they become adults. On the contrary, if they [8]**are particularly gifted in** their creative abilities, studying arts can help them further [9]**nurture their talents** and [10]**sharpen the cognitive skills**. For instance, a study suggests that students who [11]**opt for** art and musical subjects will feel more independent, [12]**boost their confidence** and [13]**become bold in decision making** when they [14]**join the workforce** in the future. Second, if some young children do not have the linguistic capabilities to clearly express themselves and communicate successfully with others, by studying art and music, they are able to [15]**convey meanings** through pictures, symbols, and rhythm. Owing to this reason, many teahcers can [16]**utilize children's artworks** to [17]**gain an insight into** what they think and feel.

In conclusion, students should [18]**strike a balance between** all subjects in an attempt to [19]**attain a healthy development** both mentally and physically. Thus, it is necessary to ensure that there is [20]**an optimum balance of** art, music, and information technology in school curricula. (360 words)

加分的 Collocations

1. **Verb + Noun** face a dilemma of　面對兩難
    = confront a dilemma of
    = be faced with a dilemma of
    = be caught in a dilemma of

2. **Verb + Noun** equip students with the ability　使學生具有⋯⋯的能力
    = provide students with the ability
    = furnish students with the ability
    = supply students with the ability

3. **Adj + Noun / Adv + Adj** of paramount importance　相當重要的
    = of critical importance
    = of crucial importance
    = of enormous importance
    = of tremendous importance
    = very important
    = critically important
    = vitally important
    = extremely important
    = particularly important

    補充 : of + **抽象名詞** = **形容詞**。

4. **Verb + Adj + Noun** earn good money　賺大錢
    = get big money
    = secure money
    = gain large money
    = get large sums of money
    = make a fortune
    = be quids in

5. **be + Adj + Preposition** be confined to... 局限於／被迫……

= be limited to

= be restricted to

= be constrained to

6. **Verb + Noun** update one's savvy 更新知識

= renew knowledge

= upgrade know-how

7. **verb + Noun + Prepoition** get a leg up on others 優於其他人

= have an advantage over others

8. **Adv + Adj** be particularly gifted in... 相當有……天賦的

= be exceptionally talented in

= be prodigiously skilled in/at

= be supremely able to

9. **Verb + Noun** nurture one's talents 培養天賦

= cultivate their talents

= foster their talents

= develop their talents

10. **Verb + Noun** sharpen the cognitive skills 提升認知能力

= improve the cognitive skills

= polish the cognitive skills

= brush up on the cognitive skills

= hone the cognitive skills

= refine the cognitive skills

= upgrade the cognitive skills

= master the cognitive skills

11. **Verb + Preposition** opt for 選擇
= choose
= select
= pick
= go for

12. **Verb + Noun** boost one's confidence 增加信心
= increase their confidence
= bolster their confidence
= boost their confidence
= build (up) their confidence
= enhance their confidence
= improve their confidence
= lift their confidence
= raise their confidence

13. **Verb + Adj** become bold in decision making 勇敢做決定
= become brave in decision making
= become courageous in decision making
= become intrepid in decision making
= become audacious in decision making

14. **Verb + Noun** join the workforce 進入職場
= enter the workforce

15. **Verb + Noun** convey meanings 表達意義
= deliver meanings

16. **Verb + Noun** utilize children's artworks （善加）利用小孩的藝術品
= use children's artworks
= exploit children's artworks
= make use of children's artworks

17. **Verb + Noun + Preposition** gain an insight into...　深入了解……

= get a considerable insight into

= obtain a detailed insight into

18. **Verb + Noun + Preposition** strike a balance between　取得平衡

= find a balance between

= achieve a balance between

= create a balance between

19. **Verb + Noun** attain a healthy development　得到健全的發展

= get a healthy development

= obtain a healthy development

20. **Adj + Noun** an optimum balance　最佳的平衡

= an ideal balance

= a perfect balance

= a proper balance

= a right balance

 心得筆記

Day 5　Environment

Although many people value their public parks, this space could be better used for other purposes such as residential areas for the evergrowing population or to develop business and boost economies.

To what extent do you agree or disagree with this statement?

大綱式寫作步驟解析

1. 閱讀題目，劃出分歧（破解題目）：

Although many people value their **public parks**, this space could be better used for **other purposes** such as residential areas for the evergrowing population or to develop business and boost economies.

* 分歧點： public parks vs. other purposses

2. 擬定大綱，確定結構：

第一段 : While **public parks, residential areas/boost economies**

第二段 : **public parks**

第三段 : **residential areas/boost economies**

第四段 : paraphrase your thesis

3. 參考範文／網路文章，找出論點：

2nd paragraph	
Subject:	beneficial for inhabitants
Argument:	promote community wellness + clean the air

Supporting Ideas:	a. promote community wellness
	  as an escape from indoor + sedentary lifestyles
	  (1) individuals' health
	  (2) the well-being of a community
	
	  when get outside + be active
	  (1) improve their health physically + psychologically
	  (2) create close-knit communities
	  (3) make the neighborhoods more appealing places
	
	b. clean the air
	  air pollution from vehicles + industry may reach
	  dangerous levels
	
	  trees combat this thorny problem
	  ← each acre of trees can remove 80 pounds of pollution
	  ← use carbon dioxide to perform photosynthesis
	  → taking it out of the atmosphere + helping to reduce
	    climate change

C
H
A
P
T
E
R

④

3rd paragraph	
Subject:	space for residential areas
Argument:	afford more job vacancies + kick-start the economy

Supporting Ideas:	a. use parks
	    (1) stage a wide variety of events (music festivals + job fairs)
	    (2) encourage local shops + restaurants to sell their merchandise
	    → not only create more jobs
	    → but benefit local business as well
	
	b. inadequate space
	    → really affect their productivity and profits
	    e.g. recent research:
	    inadequate space in offices
	    → the performance of employees ↓ by 10%
	
	    spacious business establishments
	    → bring about economic profits + prosperity of the countries

4. 看著大綱，完成文章。

Some people believe the world population increases [1]**at an alarming rate** and thus gaining access to parks is indispensable for [2]**civil residents**, but others argue this space should be utilized for economic reasons. While it is undeniable that green space in cities [3]**plays a pivotal role in** people's lives, I think such properties can be used to create [4]**job opportunities** and [5]**stimulate the local economy**.

Undoubtedly, green parks are beneficial for inhabitants to [6]**promote community wellness** and clean the air. First, if people are [7]**furnished** with parks as an escape from indoor and sedentary lifestyles, it is of great use to individuals' health and to the well-being of a community. When people can get outside and be active, city parks and open space improve their health physically and psychologically, create [8]**close-knit communities**, and make the neighborhoods more appealing places. Moreover, in urban areas, air pollution emitted from vehicles and industry may reach dangerous levels. Planting trees can [9]**combat this thorny problem** because each acre of trees can remove 80 pounds of pollution. In addition to [10]**tackling pollution**, trees and green spaces also use carbon dioxide to [11]**perform photosynthesis**, thereby taking it out of the atmosphere and helping to [12]**reduce climate change**.

Nevertheless, I still believe the areas should be better utilized to afford more job vacancies and kick-start the economy. The governments can use the parks to [13]**stage a wide variety of events** such as music festivals and job fairs or encourage local shops and restaurants to sell their merchandise during the events. This would not only create more jobs but [14]**benefit local business** as well. Also, office workers in cities [15]**are faced with the problem** of inadequate space, which really affects their productivity and profits. For instance, [16]**recent research reveals that** employees' [17]**performance rating falls** by 10% in inadequate office space. Thus, spacious business establishments will [18]**bring about** better economic profits and prosperity of the countries.

In conclusion, it is no doubt that public parks are of paramount importance to residents' communities, but I think the construction of new buildings and houses in the areas of parks is highly beneficial because it can [19]**address the issue** of insufficient workspace and [20]**accelerate economic growth**. (364 words)

加分的 Collocations

1. **Preposition + Adj + Noun** at an alarming rate　以驚人的速度
= at a fast rate
= at a rapid rate
= at a phenomenal rate

2. **Noun + Noun** civil residents　市民、居民
= dwellers
= inhabitants
= occupiers
= denizen

3. **Verb + Noun** play a pivotal role in...　在……扮演重要的角色
= occupy a vital role in people's lives
= perform a dominant role in people's lives
= serve an important role in people's lives
= have a decisive role in people's lives

4. **Noun + Noun** job opportunities　工作機會、職缺
= employment opportunities
= job vacancies
= posts

5. **Verb + Noun** stimulate the local economy　刺激當地經濟
= boost the local economy
= reinvigorate the local economy
= revive the local economy
= stimulate the local economy
= strengthen the local economy
= expand the local economy
= kick-start the local economy

6. **Verb + Noun** promote community wellness　促進社區健康
= advocate community wellness
= develop community wellness

7. **Verb + Noun** furnish sb with sth　提供某人某物
= provide sb with sth
= supply sb with sth
= offer sb sth
= afford sb sth
= grant sb sth
= give sb sth

補充：offer/afford/grant/give 是授與動詞，後面可以連續加上兩個名詞，
不需要介系詞 with。

8. **Adj + Noun** close-knit communities　關係緊密的社區
= tight-knit communities
= close communities
= cohesive communities

9. **Verb + Noun** combat this thorny problem　解決棘手／困難的問題
= address this difficult problem
= attack this complex problem
= approach this complicated problem
= come to grips with this knotty problem
= get to grips with this big problem
= grapple with this great problem
= cope with this grave problem
= deal with this pressing problem
= handle this urgent problem
= tackle this acute problem

10. **Verb + Noun** tackle pollution　解決污染

= combat pollution

= control pollution

= fight pollution

11. **Verb + Noun** perform photosynthesis　行光合作用

= do photosynthesis

12. **Verb + Noun** reduce climate change　減緩氣候變遷

= lessen climate change

13. **Verb + Noun** stage a wide variety of events　舉辦各式各樣的活動

= hold a vast variety of events

= organize an infinite variety of events

14. **Verb + Noun** benefit local business　對當地商業有幫助

= do good to local business

= promote local business

15. **Verb + Noun** be faced with the problem　面臨／遭遇問題

= be confronted with the problem

= be dogged by the problem

= be fraught with the problem

= confront the problem

= face the problem

= encounter the problem

= run into the problem

16. **Noun + Verb** recent research reveals　最近的研究顯示

= recent research shows

= recent research exhibits

= recent research demonstrates

= recent research points out

= recent research suggests

17. **Noun + Verb** performance rating falls　工作績效下降
= performance rating dips
= performance rating goes down

18. **Verb + Preposition + Noun** bring about better economic profits　產生更好經濟效益
= contribute to better economic profits
= result in better economic profits
= cause better economic profits
= give rise to better economic profits
= bring about better economic profits
= lead to better economic profits

19. **Verb + Noun** address the issue　解決問題／議題
= deal with the issue
= cope with the issue
= grapple with the issue
= tackle the issue
= handle the issue

20. **Verb + Noun** accelerate economic growth　加速經濟成長
= speed up economic growth
= expedite economic growth

Day 6　Family & Children

The family has a great influence on children's development, but the influence from outside the home plays a bigger part in children's life.

To what extent do you agree or disagree with this statement??

大綱式寫作步驟解析

1. 閱讀題目，劃出分歧（破解題目）：

The **family** has a great influence on children's development, but **the influence from outside the home** plays a bigger part in children's life.

　* 分歧點：family vs. the influence outside the home

2. 擬定大綱，確定結構：

第一段 : While **family, the influence outside the home**

第二段 : **family**

第三段 : **the influence outside the home**

第四段 : paraphrase your thesis

3. 參考範文／網路文章，找出論點：

<table>
<tr><td colspan="2" align="center">2nd paragraph</td></tr>
<tr><td>Subject:</td><td>family influence</td></tr>
<tr><td>Argument:</td><td>family influence attaches certain importance to children's life</td></tr>
<tr><td>Supporting Ideas:</td><td>Parents are indispensable + lays the foundation for
    (1) children's educational
    (2) intellectual
    (3) psychological development

e.g. parents serve as a role model + inculcate core values of the society into their children
    (1) emulate what their parents do
    (2) develop their confidence, socialisation skills, morals, + values
    (3) learn the ability to distinguish right from wrong

X wrong methods of parenting do harm to children's growth
    If juniors severely and even violently
    (1) tend to rebellious
    (2) hard to control
    → an adolescent crisis + juvenile delinquency</td></tr>
</table>

3rd paragraph	
Subject:	external influence
Argument:	external influences have more influence

Supporting Ideas:	a. schoolteachers impart + instill knowledge systematically
	    (1) make remarkable progress in academics
	    (2) prepare for their future careers
	
	    teachers are students' role models
	    (1) guiding them
	    (2) correcting their mistakes
	
	b. schools are a close-knit community where children live + study with their peers
	    (1) learn how to interact positively with others
	    (2) settle a dispute
	    (3) devote themselves to the community
	
	c. if peers set an ideal example + help children abide by correct rules
	    → classmates greatly affect children's conduct
	    (1) not only foster children's personality
	    (2) but also better their ability to regulate their conduct

4. 看著大綱，完成文章。

Every child is deeply influenced by multiple factors in his or her growth, regardless of domestic or environmental ones. While it is undeniable that parents and siblings [1]**exert a far-reaching effect on** children's development, I think other factors outside the home affect them much more.

Undoubtedly, family influence [2]**attaches certain importance to** children's life. Parents are indispensable in children's early years because their education lays the foundation for children's educational, intellectual, and psychological development. For example, parents [3]**serve as a role model** and [4]**inculcate core values of the society into their children**. Then, they may [5]**emulate what their parents do**, develop their confidence, socialisation skills, morals, plus values, and learn the ability to [6]**distinguish right from wrong**. However, wrong methods of parenting may [7]**do harm to** children's growth. If parents treat juniors severely and even violently, children [8]**tend to be rebellious** and hard to control, which can give rise to an adolescent crisis and [9]**juvenile delinquency**.

Nevertheless, I still believe external influences have more influence on their development than parents do. First and foremost, schoolteachers [10]**impart and instill knowledge of various subjects** systematically so that children can [11]**make remarkable progress in** academics and prepare for their future careers. Teachers are also expected to be students' role models, guiding them and [12]**correcting their mistakes**. Second, schools are a close-knit community where children spend most of time living and studying together with their peers from different backgrounds. This experience is of paramount importance in children's growth in that they can learn how to interact positively with others, [13]**settle a dispute** and [14]**devote themselves to** the community. Finally, classmates can also greatly affect children's conduct if peers can [15]**set an ideal example** and help children [16]**abide by correct rules**. This experience can not only [17]**foster children's personality**, but also [18]**better their ability** to [19]**regulate their conduct**.

[20]**To conclude**, although it is clear that the family plays a pivotal role, I would argue that it is outside social factors that can provide a supportive, secure, and nurturing environment to help a child become a responsible adult. (342 words)

1. **Verb + Adj + Noun** exert a far-reaching effect on 影響很深遠
= have a profound effect on
= produce a powerful effect on
= bring about a strong effect on
= show a significant effect on

2. **Verb + Noun** attach certain importance to... 認為……相當重要
= place certain importance to
= stress certain importance to

3. **Verb + Noun** serve as a role model 作為榜樣
= function as a role model
= set a good example
= show a shining example

4. **Verb + Noun** inculcate core values of the society into sb 灌輸社會核心價值給某人
= instill core values of the society into their children
= drum core values of the society into their children
= drill core values of the society into their children

5. **Verb + Noun** emulate what their parents do 仿效父母的行為
= imitate what their parents do
= follow what their parents do
= copy what their parents do
= mimic what their parents do
= model themselves on what their parents do
= pattern themselves on what their parents do

6. **Verb + Noun** distinguish right from wrong　分辨對錯
=   tell right from wrong
=   differentiate right from wrong

7. **Verb + Noun** do harm to...　對……有害
=   cause serious harm to
=   inflict untold harm to

8. **Verb + Infinitive** tend to V　容易做……
=   be likely to V
=   apt to V

9. **Adj + Noun** juvenile delinquency　青少年犯罪
=   adolescent crime
=   teen's wrongdoing

10. **Verb + Noun** impart and instill knowledge of...　傳遞並灌輸……的知識
=   convey and inculcate knowledge of various subjects

11. **Verb + Adj + Noun** make remarkable progress in　進步很多
=   achieve substantial progress in

12. **Verb + Noun** correct one's mistakese　改正某人的錯誤
=   rectify one's mistakes

13. **Verb + Noun** settle a dispute　解決糾紛
=   resolve a dispute
=   solve a dispute

14. **Verb + Noun + Preposition** devote oneself to...　奉獻自己於……
=   dedicate themselves to

15. **Verb + Noun** set an ideal example 樹立完美的典範

= hold sb/sth up as a perfect example

16. **Verb + Noun** abide by correct rules 遵守正確的規範

= obey correct rules

= follow correct rules

= comply with correct rules

= conform to correct rules

= stick to correct rules

= adhere to correct rules

17. **Verb + Noun** foster children's personality 培養小孩的人格

= develop children's personality

= nurture children's personality

18. **Verb + Noun** better one's ability 改善某人的能力

= improve their ability

= enhance their ability

= advance their ability

= ameliorate their ability

19. **Verb + Noun** regulate one's conduct 規範某人的行為

= control their behavior

20. To conclude, ... 總結來說

= In conclusion, ...

= To sum up, ...

Day 7　Media & Advertising

Some people say that advertising encourages us to buy things that we really do not need. Others say that advertisements tell us about new products that may improve our lives.

Which viewpoint do you agree with?

(大綱式寫作步驟解析)

1. 閱讀題目，劃出分歧（破解題目）：

Some people say that advertising encourages us to **buy things that we really do not need**. Others say that advertisements tell us about **new products that may improve our lives**.

* 分歧點：buy things we do not need vs. new products that improve our lives

2. 擬定大綱，確定結構：

第一段：While **buy things we do not need, new products that improve our lives**

第二段：**buy things we do not need**

第三段：**new products that improve our lives**

第四段：paraphrase your thesis

3. 參考範文／網路文章，找出論點：

2nd paragraph	
Subject:	advertisement = scam
Argument:	encourages consumers to purchase expensive + unnecessary things
Supporting Ideas:	use celebrities to (1) influence their followers' choices (2) promote brands (3) increase sales figures → create fake demands for the product + exaggerate the benefits e.g. buying alcohol = is injurious to health urge people to buy them ← become rejuvenated after drinking it → ad take good advantage of consumers' needs

3rd paragraph	
Subject:	new products that improve our lives
Argument:	beneficial for both consumers + companies
Supporting Ideas:	a. looking for a wide variety of choices $\rightarrow$ their life more efficient + comfortable e.g. the turnover of Apple company's new mobiles (iPhone 13) $\uparrow$ $\leftarrow$ the latest application info (like iOS 15.2) b. inform their customers: newly upgraded products $\leftarrow$ cut-throat competition of gaining the market share Ads help (1) gain popularity of their products (2) increase their market share $\leftarrow$ reaching a potential customer consumers + companies depend heavily on the ad $\leftarrow$ complete the purpose $\leftarrow$ a strong correlation (advertisements + people for growth in trade + lives)

4. 看著大綱，完成文章。

Advertising, for national and international companies, functions as [1]**marketing tactics to** [2]**promote their products** to the world. While some believe that advertisements [3]**lure people** into [4]**purchasing their merchandise** which is not necessary, I think that they provide us with new items which [5]**enhance our lives**.

Interestingly, some people argue that the advertisement is [6]**the biggest scam** because it often encourages consumers to purchase things which are expensive and unnecessary. Some companies use celebrities to influence their followers' choices, promote brands, and increase sales figures. These influences create fake demands for the product and [7]**exaggerate the benefits** for using the products. For instance, some promotions like buying alcohol, which [8]**is injurious to health**, **urge people** to buy them because after drinking the alcohol, people may become rejuvenated. Therefore, advertisements [9]**take good advantage of consumers' needs** as a tool to sell unnecessary and costly products.

[10]**On the flip side**, I still believe adverts are extremely beneficial for both consumers and companies. From consumers' perspectives, people are looking for [11]**a wide variety of choices** to make their life more efficient and comfortable. For example, the turnover of Apple company's new mobiles, iPhone 13, is rising because of the adverts, which offers the latest application information, like iOS 15.2, to all customers, who are always looking for updated Apple products. From companies' angle, companies also need to [12]**inform their customers about their newly upgraded products**. The promotion of the product plays an essential role in the era of the 21st century because there is [13]**cut-throat competition** between the companies to gain the market share. Advertisements will help the companies to [14]**gain popularity** of their products among its customers and thus to increase their market share by [15]**reaching a potential customer**. As a result, both consumers and companies [16]**depend heavily on** the advertisement to [17]**complete the purpose** since there is [18]**a strong correlation between** advertisements and people for growth in trade and lives.

In conclusion, advertisements can [19]**be both a boon and a bane**. They may persuade people to purchase things that are not necessarily required, but they perform a key role in updating customers on [20]**state-of-the-art product information**. (354 words)

加分的 Collocations

1. **Adj + Noun** marketing tactics　行銷策略
= marketing strategies
= marketing policies
= marketing campaigns
= marketing schemes
= marketing maneuvers

2. **Verb + Noun** promote their products　宣傳產品
= advertise their products

3. **Verb + Noun + Preposition** lure sb into V-ing　誘惑某人做……
= entice sb into V-ing
= persuade sb into V-ing

4. **Verb + Noun** purchase their merchandise　購買商品
= buy their goods
= buy their commodities
= buy their products

5. **Verb + Noun** enhance our lives　幫助我們的生活
= help our lives
= facilitate our lives
= improve our lives
= enrich our lives

6. **Adj + Noun** the biggest scam　最大的詐騙
= the biggest con
= the biggest fiddle

7. | **Verb + Noun** | exaggerate the benefits　誇大效益
= overstate the benefits

8. | **be + Adj + Prepositioon + Noun** | be injurious to health　對健康有害處
= be harmful to health
= be detrimental to health
= be deleterious to health
= be damaging to health
= be dangerous to health

9. | **Verb + Noun** | take good advantage of consumers' needs　利用消費者需求
= use consumers' needs
= utilize consumers' needs

10. | **Preposition + Noun** | On the flip side　另一方面，從相反的角度來看
= On the opposite side

11. | **Adj + Noun** | a wide variety of choices　各式各樣的選擇
= an impressive variety of choices
= an endless variety of choices
= a vast variety of choices
= a large / big selection

12. | **Verb + Noun + Preposition + Noun** | inform sb about/of sth　告知某人某事
= notify their customers of their newly upgraded products

13. | **Adj + Noun** | cut-throat competition　激烈競爭
= fierce competition
= intense competition
= keen competition
= serious competition
= severe competition

= stiff competition

= strong competition

= tough competition

14. **Verb + Noun** gain (in) popularity 受到歡迎

= win popularity

= grow in popularity

15. **Verb + Noun** reach a potential customer 觸及到潛在客戶

= attract a possible customer

= entice a prospective customer

= get a potential customer

16. **Verb + Adv + Preposition** depend heavily on... 相當依賴……

= depend crucially on

= depend greatly on

17. **Verb + Noun** complete their purpose 達到目的

= accomplish their purpose

= achieve their purpose

= fulfil their purpose

18. **Adj + Noun + Preposition** a strong correlation between 高度關聯

= a close correlation between

= a high correlation between

= a remarkable correlation between

= a significant correlation between

19. **Verb + Preposition + Noun** function as both a boon and a bane 有好有壞

= serve as both benefits and blight

20. **Adj + Noun** state-of-the-art product information　最新／最先進的產品資訊

= latest product information

= newest product information

= new-fashioned product information

= up-to-date product information

= up-to-the-minute product information

= cutting-edge product information

心得筆記

Day 8　Crime & Punishment

Many offenders commit more crimes after serving their first punishment.

Why is this happening, and what measures can be taken to tackle this problem?

大綱式寫作步驟解析

1. 閱讀題目，劃出分歧（破解題目）：

Why is this happening, and **what measures can be taken to tackle this problem**?

* 分歧點： why & what measures

2. 擬定大綱，確定結構：

第一段 : While **reasons, measures**

第二段 : **reasons**

第三段 : **measures**

第四段 : paraphrase your thesis

3. 參考範文／網路文章，找出論點：

2ⁿᵈ paragraph	
Subject:	two reasons why most first-time offenders commit crimes again
Argument:	no jobs + social stigma
Supporting Ideas:	a. employers are reluctant to hire ex-offenders job opportunities 　(1) extremely challenging to find a legitimate source of income 　(2) the lack of money forces offenders to commit crimes once again b. encounter many difficulties (social stigma) 　← the society X accept them + ignore such kind of people 　→ encourage them to commit a crime again e.g. a job interview 　← their bad record 　→ companies check his/her records 　→ employers reject the profile

3rd paragraph	
Subject:	two measures
Argument:	subsidy + rehabilitation
Supporting Ideas:	a. if gov't subsidizes these criminals for at least 2-3 months 　　→ seek a job w/o worrying about overheads e.g. In developed countries, to deter ex-criminals from resorting back to the previous unethical methods of earning money 　　→ WHO provides 　　(1) $ help 　　(2) basic amenities (shelter, food + clothes) b. send people who have the impulse to hurt others to rehabilitation centres 　　(1) be counselled + treated with professional 　　　　psychologists + psychiatrists 　　(2) change their way of thinking + attitude towards life 　　→ preventing them from attempting any illicit actions

4. 看著大綱，完成文章。

It has been observed that [1]**the majority of criminals** [2]**indulge in greater illegal activities** after being released from [3]**police custody**. This essay will discuss the reasons for this development—lack of employment opportunities and the [4]**social stigma** associated with people who have [5]**committed crimes**. Fortunately, this [6]**thorny problem** could be addressed if the government takes some useful measures in time.

There are two reasons why most first-time offenders commit crimes again. First of all, because a large number of employers [7]**are reluctant to** offer ex-offenders job opportunities, it becomes extremely challenging for them to find [8]**a legitimate source of income**. Hence, the lack of money forces offenders to commit crimes once again. Secondly, when released from prison, they encounter many difficulties such as social stigma since the society do not accept them and always ignore such kind of people, which encourage them to commit a crime again. [9]**A case in point is that** owing to their bad record, whenever a person appears for a job interview, companies check his/her records, and more often than not employers are very likely to reject the profile of those people who did any criminal activity in their past.

However, those problems can be solved by two methods: subsidy and rehabilitation. First, if the government [10]**subsidizes these criminals** for at least 2-3 months after their release, they can [11]**seek a job** without worrying about [12]**enormous overheads**. In developed countries, for example, to [13]**deter ex-criminals from resorting back to** the previous [14]**unethical methods** of earning money, World Health Organisation (WHO) provides financial help and basic amenities, such as shelter, food and clothes. Another method is to send people who [15]**have the impulse to** hurt others to rehabilitation centres, where they can be counselled and treated with professional psychologists and psychiatrists. These experts may even change their way of thinking and attitude towards life, therefore preventing them from attempting any [16]**illicit actions.**

In conclusion, most of the previous [17]**hardened wrongdoers** released from prison commit crimes again [18]**on account of** unemployment and social stigma. However, the government can [19]**grapple with such issue** with [20]**monetary help** until they are employed and put them into rehab for counselling and treatment.

1. the majority of criminals　大部分的罪犯
=   most criminals

2. **Verb + Noun** indulge in greater illegal activities　涉入更嚴重的違法行為
=   be involved in greater illegal activities
=   engage in greater illegal activities
=   participate in greater illegal activities
=   take part in greater illegal activities
=   undertake greater illegal activities

3. **Noun + Noun** police custody　警方拘留
=   police detention

4. **Adj + Noun** social stigma　（社會上的）惡名／污名
=   social disgrace

5. **Verb + Noun** commit crimes　犯罪
=   carry out crimes

6. **Adj + Noun** this thorny problem　棘手的問題
=   this difficult problem
=   this complex problem
=   this complicated problem
=   this knotty problem
=   this big problem
=   this great problem
=   this grave problem
=   this pressing problem
=   this urgent problem
=   this acute problem

7. **Adv + Adj** be deeply reluctant　非常不願意

=   be remarkably unwilling to

8. **Adj + Noun** a legitimate source of income　合法／正當的收入來源

=   a legal source of income

=   a lawful source of income

=   a rightful source of income

9. A case in point is that + S + V　舉例來說

=   NP is a case in point.

=   For example, S + V

=   For instance, S + V

=   To illustrate, S + V

10. **Verb + Noun** subsidize these criminals　資助／補貼這些罪犯

=   fund these criminals

=   sponsor these criminals

=   support these criminals

11. **Verb + Noun** seek a job　找工作

=   look for a job

=   hunt for a job

12. **Adj + Noun** daily expenditure　日常花費

=   great expenses

=   vast expenditure

=   considerable payments

=   high costs

=   prohibitive charges

=   exorbitant fees

=   massive outlays

13. | **Verb + Noun + Preposition** | deter sb from V-ing　遏止某人做……

=　prevent ex-criminals from resorting back to

=　discourage ex-criminals from resorting back to

14. | **Adj + Noun** | unethical methods　不道德的方式

=　immoral methods

=　wrong methods

=　bad methods

15. | **Verb + Noun** | have the impulse to V　做……的衝動

=　have the desire to

=　have the urge to

16. | **Adj + Noun** | illicit actions　非法行為

=　illegal actions

17. | **Adj + Noun** | hardened wrongdoers　慣犯

=　habitual criminals

=　hardened offenders

=　hardened outlaws

18. on account of + NP　因為

=　because of

=　due to

=　owing to

=　thanks to

=　as a result of

19. | **Verb + Preposition + Noun** | grapple with such issue　處理這樣的問題

=　combat such issue

=　address such issue

=　attack such issue

=　approach such issue

=　come to grips with such issue

=　get to grips with such issue

=　cope with such issue

=　deal with such issue

=　handle such issue

=　tackle such issue

20. **Adj + Noun** monetary help　金錢援助

=　financial aids

=　fiscal assistance

心得筆記

Day 9　Technology

Maintaining public libraries is a waste of money since there is computer technology.

To what extent do you agree or disagree?

大綱式寫作步驟解析

1. 閱讀題目，劃出分歧（破解題目）：

Maintaining **public libraries** is a waste of money since there is **computer technology**.

* 分歧點：public libraries vs. computer technology

2. 擬定大綱，確定結構：

第一段：While, **public libraries, computer technology**

第二段：**public libraries**

第三段：**computer technology**

第四段：paraphrase your thesis

3. 參考範文／網路文章，找出論點：

2nd paragraph	
Subject:	using an online source of information via computer
Argument:	revolutionized information access + keep internet users posted on the most updated event + solve the problem of deterioration

Supporting Ideas:	a. cutting-edge computer systems revolutionized information access
	   ← vast stores of information on many worlds are accessible
	
	   digitization → store a large amount of information w/o physical boundary + time limitations = inconceivable at public libraries
	b. online electronic version of latest newspapers
	   → keep internet users posted on the most updated event
	
	   vital for individuals + corporates
	   ← gain speedy + timely access to what is happening around them
	
	c. solve the problem of deterioration
	   ← books may be subject to the risk of being damaged
	
	   X, books or documents X suffer wear and tear
	   ← the electric materials

3rd paragraph	
Subject:	public libraries
Argument:	distinguishing features which cannot be substituted by online sources
Supporting Ideas:	a. students: libraries are important for pupils 　　(1) study in libraries 　　(2) enhance their verbal communication skills 　　(3) encourage social interaction 　　(4) cement their relationship 　　(5) fully concentrate on their studies 　　← the atmosphere by the physical surroundings b. the elderly: senior citizens frequent public libraries 　　(1) not only get a platform to spend time reading books 　　　　or newspapers in a calm + pleasant environment 　　(2) but also get a feeling of togetherness 　　← knowing other older people

4. 看著大綱，完成文章。

People can easily and conveniently ¹**gain access to books,** journals and newspapers with the help of public libraries. Unfortunately, ²**with the advent and advancement in** the computer technology, ³**there is some concern about** the maintenance of public libraries. In my opinion, although technology helps us obtain information efficiently, I believe public libraries are still crucial in a way that computers cannot perform and therefore should be maintained for public access.

On the one hand, there are some advantages when using an online source of information via computer. First, the ⁴**cutting-edge computer systems** have ⁵**revolutionized information access** because ⁶**vast stores of information about many worlds** are accessible via the Internet. Through digitization, we could store a large amount of information without ⁷**physical boundary** and time limitations, which is ⁸**almost inconceivable** at any public libraries. Second, the online electronic version of latest newspapers could help internet users to ⁹**keep themselves posted on** the most updated event. This is ¹⁰**especially vital** for individuals and corporates to gain speedy and timely access to what is happening around them to be competitive. Finally, maintaining online libraries can solve the problem of deterioration. In traditional libraries, books may ¹¹**be subject to the risk** of being damaged; however, thanks to the electric materials, books or documents do not have to ¹²**suffer wear and tear**.

On the other hand, public libraries are still ¹³**irreplaceable resources** because of their ¹⁴**distinguishing features** which cannot be substituted by online sources. From students' perspective, libraries are important for pupils because they can study in libraries, enhance their verbal communication skills, encourage social interaction, and ¹⁵**cement their relationship**; most importantly, they can ¹⁶**fully concentrate on their studies** due to the atmosphere created by the physical surroundings. From the elderly's perspective, ¹⁷**senior citizens** who have retired from their professional life ¹⁸**frequent public libraries** in the city, where they not only get a platform to spend time reading books, newspapers, and magazines in a calm and pleasant environment, but also get ¹⁹**a feeling of togetherness** by knowing other older people.

In conclusion, despite [20]**the dizzying rush of technological innovations**, there is a need to spend money maintaining public libraries because of its educational place and social importance in communities. (364 words)

加分的 Collocations

1. **Verb + Noun** gain access to... 取得……（的使用權／機會）
   = get unrestricted access to books
   = get easy access to books

2. **Preposition + Noun** with the advent of... 隨著／因為……的出現
   = due to the coming and progress in
   = because of arrival and development in

3. **Noun + Preposition** there is some concern about... 對……有顧慮／疑慮
   = there is some worry about
   = there is some fear about
   = there is some apprehension about

4. **Adj + Noun** cutting-edge computer systems 最新／創新的電腦系統
   = bleeding-edge computer systems
   = leading-edge computer systems
   = state-of-the-art computer systems
   = groundbreaking computer systems
   = revolutionary computer systems
   = innovative computer systems
   = pioneering computer systems

5. **Verb + Noun** revolutionize information access 革新資訊的獲取
   = change information access
   = transform information access
   = reform information access
   = modernize information access

6. **Adj + Noun** a considerable amount of... 大量的……
= considerable stores of information on/about many worlds
= good stores of information on/about many worlds
= great stores of information on/about many worlds
= large stores of information on/about many worlds
= inexhaustible stores of information on/about many worlds
= a massive amount of information on/about many worlds
= a substantial amount of information on/about many worlds

7. **Adj + Noun** physical boundary 物理（空間）限制
= physical limitation

8. **Adv + Adj** almost inconceivable 幾乎無法想像的
= nearly unbelievable
= virtually incredible
= practically implausible

9. **Verb + Noun** keep oneself posted on... 獲得／跟上最新……的資訊
= update themselves on
= keep up with
= keep abreast of

10. **Adv + Adj** especially vital 特別重要
= particularly important
= particularly crucial

11. **Adj + Preposition + Noun** be subject to the risk 遭受風險
= be vulnerable to the risk
= be susceptible to the risk
= subject sb to the risk

12. **Verb + Noun** suffer wear and tear　遭受磨損

= experience wear and tear

= endure wear and tear

13. **Adj + Noun** irreplaceable resources　無法取代的／獨一無二的資源

= unique resources

= one-of-a-kind resources

14. **Adj + Noun** distinguishing features　顯著的特色

= distinctive features

= peculiar features

= characteristic features

= conspicuous features

= dominant features

= notable features

= noteworthy features

= noticeable features

= predominant features

= prominent features

15. **Verb + Noun** cement their relationship　強化關係

= improve their relationship

= strengthen their relationship

= reinforce their relationship

16. **Adv + Verb + Preposition** fully concentrate on...　完全集中精神在……

= entirely focus on

17. **Adj + Noun** senior citizens　年長者

= the elderly

= the aged

18. **Verb + Noun** frequent public libraries　經常去公共圖書館

= frequently visit public libraries

= frequently go to public libraries

19. **Noun + Preposition + Noun** a feeling of togetherness　和睦相處的感覺

= a feeling of closeness

20. **Adj + Noun** the dizzying rush of technological innovations　太快且令人困惑的科技創新

= the dizzying pace of technological innovations

= the confusing haste of technological innovations

= the bewildering speed of technological innovations

心得筆記

Day 10　Business & Money

Today different types of robots are being developed which can serve as companions and workers to help at work and at home.

Is this a positive or negative development?

(大綱式寫作步驟解析)

1. 閱讀題目，劃出分歧（破解題目）：

Is this a **positive** or **negative** development?

* 分歧點：positive development vs. negative development

2. 擬定大綱，確定結構：

第一段：While **positive, negative**

第二段：**positive**

第三段：**negative**

第四段：paraphrase your thesis

3. 參考範文／網路文章，找出論點：

	2nd paragraph
Subject:	positive
Argument:	improve productivity + perform multitasking

Supporting Ideas:	a. In workplace, machines can tackle repetitive, tedious tasks
	   → the introduction of automation into manufacturing processes
	   (1) less manual delays
	   (2) optimal machine efficiency
	   (3) increased manual productivity
	   staff members are rendered the opportunity to work in other areas + will create a better environment
	   → their work efficiency + efficacy improve
	   → extremely satisfied clients
	
	b. At home, machines equipped with intelligent technology
	   → make life increasingly easy + effortless
	
	   e.g.
	   (1) their robot vacuum cleaners are doing chores
	   (2) people relax after a long day of work
	   (3) parents have an opportunity to savor the precious moment with their kids
	
	   Also, robots
	   (1) help maneuver disabled people
	   (2) serve as companions to the elderly

3rd paragraph	
Subject:	negative
Argument:	unhealthy lifestyle + unemployment
Supporting Ideas:	a. e.g. in the past, be healthy + stay fit 　← doing numerous house chores 　(1) doing the laundry 　(2) cleaning the floor 　(3) washing dishes 　X the total dependence on + replacement of household 　　gadgets 　→ X get enough physical exercise to maintain a healthy 　　body b. people (doing mundane tasks) are losing their jobs 　← robotics + excessive reliance on automation 　← are less error-prone than humans 　→ have eradicated a wide range of jobs, especially 　　manufacturing + banking 　→ a surge in unemployment

4. 看著大綱，完成文章。

These days, a wide variety of robots or artificial intelligence (AI) are invented to help us work more efficiently and effectively at an office or at home. Nevertheless, while there are advantages associated with the use of automation or AI, [1]**overdependence on machines and robots** is [2]**a negative indication** for individuals and our society as a whole.

Despite the [3]**hectic schedules and pace of city life**, AI or robots can help us improve productivity and [4]**perform multitasking**. In the workplace, because machines can [5]**tackle repetitive, tedious tasks**, the introduction of automation into manufacturing processes has many different productivity benefits, such as less manual delays, [6]**optimal machine efficiency**, and [7]**increased manual productivity**. In other words, staff members [8]**are rendered the opportunity** to work in other areas and will create a better environment for the business as a whole. With more energy and focus into their work, their work efficiency and efficacy can improve, which will also lead to extremely [9]**satisfied clients**. At home, machines [10]**equipped with intelligent technology** make life [11]**increasingly easy and effortless** for families. For example, while their robot vacuum cleaners are [12]**doing chores** at home, people can finally relax after a long day of work or parents can have an opportunity to [13]**savor the precious moment** with their kids. Also, robots are even able to perform functions to help maneuver disabled people or [14]**serve as companions** to the elderly.

However, overuse and over-dependence of machines can bring about an unhealthy lifestyle and unemployment. To illustrate, in the past, people used to be healthy and [15]**stay fit** by doing numerous house chores like doing the laundry, cleaning the floor and washing dishes, but with the total dependence on and replacement of household gadgets, they don't get enough physical exercise to [16]**maintain a healthy body**. In addition, due to robotics and excessive reliance on automation, many people who were responsible for doing mundane tasks are losing their jobs. Because robots [17]**are less error-prone** than humans, they have [18]**eradicated a wide range of jobs** in several industries, especially manufacturing and banking, thereby resulting in [19]**a surge in unemployment**.

In conclusion, although there are many advantages of using machines, over-reliance on AI can lead to decrease in physical fitness and job loss, which will emerge as a great challenge to the society [20]**in the foreseeable future**. (384 words)

加分的 Collocations

1. **Noun + Preposition** overdependence on... 過度依賴……
= over-reliance on machines and robots

2. **Adj + Noun** a negative indication 負面的跡象
= a bad indication

3. **Adj + Noun** hectic schedules and pace of city life 繁忙的活動和城市生活步調
= busy schedules and pace of city life
= hustle and bustle of city life

4. **Verb + Noun** perform multitasking 執行多工（同步執行不同事項）
= carry out multitasking
= do multitasking
= fulfil multitasking

5. **Verb + Adj + Noun** tackle repetitive, tedious tasks 處理重複且無聊的任務
= do repetitious, boring tasks
= perform repetitive, monotonous tasks

6. **Adj + Noun** optimal machine efficiency 機器最佳效率
= optimum machine efficiency
= best machine efficiency

7. **Adj + Noun** increased manual productivity 增加的人工產能
= improved manual output
= greater manual production

8. **Verb + Noun** be rendered the opportunity　得到機會
= be given the opportunity
= be offered the opportunity
= be granted the opportunity
= be afforded the opportunity
= be provided with the opportunity

9. **Adj + Noun** satisfied clients　滿意的客戶
= pleased clients

10. **Verb + Preposition** be equipped with...　附有／配有……
= be installed with intelligent technology
= be outfitted with intelligent technology
= be supplied with intelligent technology
= be furnished with intelligent technology

11. **Adv + Adj** increasingly easy and effortless　越來越簡單且輕鬆
= more and more easy and effortless

12. **Verb + Noun** do chores　做家事
= carry out chores

13. **Verb + Noun** savor the precious moment　享受珍貴時刻
= enjoy the precious moment
= relish the precious moment
= appreciate the precious moment

14. **Verb + Preposition + Noun** serve as companions　當作陪伴者
= function as companions

15. **Verb + Adj** stay fit　保持好身材
= keep fit
= keep in shape

16. **Verb + Noun** maintain a healthy body　維持健康身體

= keep a healthy body

= stay a healthy body

= remain a healthy body

17. be less error-prone　比較不會出錯

= be less disposed to

= be less predisposed to

= be less susceptible to

18. **Verb + Noun** eradicate a wide range of jobs　消除／滅各式各樣的工作（機會）

= eliminate a wide range of jobs

= exterminate a wide range of jobs

= wipe out a wide range of jobs

= stamp out a wide range of jobs

19. **Noun + Preposition** a surge in unemployment　失業率急遽上升

= a rise in unemployment

= a growth in unemployment

= an increase in unemployment

= a climb in unemployment

20. **Adj + Noun** in the foreseeable future　在不遠的將來

= in the not-too-distant future

= in the near future

= in the foreseeable future

= in the immediate future

Day 11　Communication & Personality

Being a celebrity – such as a famous film star or sports personality – brings problems as well as benefits.

Do you think that being celebrity brings more benefits or more problems?

大綱式寫作步驟解析

1. 閱讀題目，劃出分歧（破解題目）：

Being a celebrity – such as a famous film star or sports personality – brings **problems** as well as **benefits**.

* **分歧點**：benefits vs. problems

2. 擬定大綱，確定結構：

第一段 : While **benefits, problems**

第二段 : **benefits**

第三段 : **problems**

第四段 : paraphrase your thesis

3. 參考範文／網路文章，找出論點：

2nd paragraph	
Subject:	benefits
Argument:	getting more opportunities + earning wealth
Supporting Ideas:	a. gains fame → have access to more opportunities
	e.g. outstanding basketball players end up becoming the face of popular sporting brands, such as Michael Jordan + Nike some actors dive into new businesses: opening a perfume / clothing store w/o doubt, becoming famous opens multiple doors: have never been done without the fame b. fame → brings lots of fortune celebrities + famous people rich > the average Joe convert a dream to a reality: (1) luxurious homes + cars (2) fancy gifts (3) expensive clothes (4) materialistic pleasures of life

3rd paragraph	
Subject:	problems
Argument:	a privacy violation + constantly and harshly judge celebrities
Supporting Ideas:	a. a privacy violation 　← under public surveillance 　(1) they X go around 　(2) do things at will 　(3) are afraid of getting surrounded by stans 　(4) being forced to have a picture or an autograph 　are under public scrutiny 　← paparazzi is a constant nuisance + breaches their 　　privacy 　→ their private secrets go viral b. constantly + harshly judge celebrities via magazines, newspapers + blogs 　(1) their personalities 　(2) habits 　(3) bodies 　reading demeaning, insulting, + derogatory criticism = 　part + parcel of a celebrity's daily routine 　= live in a life (millions of people talk behind his/her 　back)

4. 看著大綱，完成文章。

Nowadays, celebrities, such as [1]**renowned actors** or sports players, [2]**are strongly supported** and [3]**fiercely criticized** both in public forums and on social media. While being [4]**a showbiz or sporting celebrity** has its benefits, I personally believe that the problems do outweigh the advantages.

Admittedly, there are two main advantages to being famous: getting more opportunities and earning wealth. When people [5]**gain fame**, they have access to more opportunities related to their career. For instance, several [6]**outstanding basketball players** end up becoming the face of popular sporting brands, such as Michael Jordan's teaming up with Nike. Additionally, some actors [7]**dive into new businesses**, such as opening a perfume or clothing store. Without a doubt, becoming famous opens multiple doors, which could have never been done without the fame. The other advantage of being famous is that fame generally brings lots of fortune. Celebrities and other famous people are generally richer than the [8]**average Joe**. Luxurious homes and cars, fancy gifts, expensive clothes and other [9]**materialistic pleasures of life** convert a dream to a reality when people become celebrities.

However, there are disadvantages to be considered for being a superstar. Firstly, celebrities often face [10]**a privacy violation** as they are always [11]**under public scrutiny**. Once they become public figures, that means they cannot go around and do things [12]**at will**. They are afraid of getting surrounded by [13]**stans** or being forced to [14]**pose for a picture** or sign an autograph. Moreover, paparazzi are regared as a constant nuisance and [15]**breach their privacy**, and therefore sometimes their private secrets [16]**go viral** through the news reports or social networking sites. Secondly, people [17]**constantly and harshly judge** celebrities on their personalities, habits, and bodies via magazines, newspapers, blogs, and other forms of media. Reading [18]**demeaning, insulting, and derogatory criticism** is part and parcel of a celebrity's [19]**daily routine**. In other words, celebrities have no choice but to live a life in which millions of people talk behind their back on a daily basis.

In conclusion, popularity brings advantages of gaining worldwide fame and getting heaps of money, but I believe that celebrated figures are faced with more problems—an invasion of privacy and [20]**vicious verbal attack**. (361 words)

加分的 Collocations

1. **Adj + Noun** renowned actors　有名的演員
= famous actors
= well-known actors
= celebrated actors
= popular actors
= established actors

2. **Adv + Verb** be strongly supported　非常／大力支持
= be fervently supported
= be overwhelmingly supported

3. **Adv + Verb** fiercely criticize　猛烈抨擊
= bitterly criticize
= heavily criticize
= roundly criticize
= severely criticize
= sharply criticize
= strongly criticize

4. **Noun + Noun** a showbiz or sporting celebrity　娛樂圈或體體育界名人
= a showbiz or sporting figure
= a showbiz or sporting icon
= a showbiz or sporting star

5. **Verb + Noun** gain fame　成名
= achieve fame
= come to fame
= find fame
= rise to fame
= shoot to fame
= win fame

6. **Adj + Noun** outstanding basketball players　出色的籃球員

= brilliant basketball players

= exceptional basketball players

= excellent basketball players

= superb basketball players

= fantastic basketball players

= terrific basketball players

= wonderful basketball players

7. **Verb + Preposition + Noun** dive into new businesses　從事新行業

= dive in new businesses

= start up new businesses

= set up new businesses

8. **Adj + Noun** average Joe　一般人

= average Jane

= ordinary Joe

= ordinary Jane

= an ordinary person

= Joe Bloggs

= Joe Blow

9. **Adj + Noun** materialistic pleasures of life　拜金的物質生活

= money-oriented pleasures of life

10. **Noun + Noun** a privacy violation　隱私侵犯

= a privacy intrusion

= a privacy invasion

= an invasion of privacy

= an intrusion on one's privacy

= a privacy breach

11. **Preposition + Adj + Noun** under public scrutiny　受到大眾監視／監督
=　under public surveillance
=　under public inspection
=　under public supervision

12. **Preposition + Noun** at will　任意地
=　at one's pleasure
=　at one's discretion

13. **Adj + Noun** stans（= stalker + fan）　瘋狂粉絲
=　loyal fans
=　adoring fans
=　ardent fans
=　avid fans
=　big fans
=　dedicated fans
=　devoted fans
=　great fans
=　keen fans

14. **Verb + Preposition + Noun** pose for a picture　擺姿勢拍照
=　adopt a pose for a picture
=　assume a pose for a picture
=　strike a pose for a picture

15. **Verb + Noun** breach one's privacy　侵犯某人隱私
=　disturb their privacy
=　intrude on their privacy
=　invade their privacy
=　violate their privacy

16. **Verb + Adj** go viral　瘋傳

17. **Adv + Verb** constantly and harshly judge sb　一直嚴厲批評某人
= persistently bitterly judge sb
= frequently and severely judge sb

18. **Adj + Noun** demeaning, insulting, and derogatory criticism　貶低、羞辱人且毀謗的批評
= bitter, fierce, and trenchant criticism
= severe, sharp, and strident criticism
= harsh, adverse, and damaging criticism
= damning, hostile, and scathing criticism

19. **Adj + Noun** daily routine　日常慣例
= everyday routine
= day-to-day routine
= regular routine
= per diem routine

20. **Adj + Noun** vicious verbal attack　惡毒的言語攻擊
= mean spoken attack
= hurtful verbal attack
= malicious verbal attack
= nasty verbal attack
= spiteful verbal attack

Day 12　Government

A government has a responsibility to its citizens to ensure their safety. Therefore, some people think that the government should increase spending on defense but spend less on social benefits.

To what extent do you agree or disagree?

(大綱式寫作步驟解析)

1. 閱讀題目，劃出分歧（破解題目）：

Therefore, some people think that the government should increase spending on **defense** but spend less on **social benefits**.

* 分歧點： defense vs. social benefits

2. 擬定大綱，確定結構：

第一段 : While **defense, benefits**

第二段 : **defense**

第三段 : **social benefits**

第四段 : paraphrase your thesis

3. 參考範文／網路文章，找出論點：

2nd paragraph	
Subject:	defense
Argument:	strengthen a country's security + combat international terrorism
Supporting Ideas:	a. lays a firm foundation to a country stability: nations are not on good terms ← territorial / economic issues
	X, bad relation escalates into a full-scale war in an instant
	X, if builds powerful military forces (1) win the respect of its neighboring countries (2) become the leader of the region (3) more beneficial terms in international agreements
	b. combat international terrorism: e.g. Iran (1) face grave threats (2) experience terrorist attacks
	increasing police force (1) reduce threats from terrorists (2) nip them in the bud

3rd paragraph	
Subject:	social benefits
Argument:	social prosperity is as critical as the military
Supporting Ideas:	budget on military expansion X at the expense of social welfare ← social prosperity is = critical = military = services (education, medical services / transportation) be subsidized Gov't ensure people meet their basic needs (food, shelter + health) ← a dearth of social benefits can inflict a massive damage to a country's residents e.g. North Korea strongly emphasizes the development of military → only to create a poverty-stricken country The country's terrible suffering ← the deficiency of social benefit programs (retirement schemes, disability benefits + subsidized housing) → resentment among the disadvantaged → social uprising against the authorities X, offered welfare for the neediest through various plans (1) raise their living standards (2) helping its people become happy + contented

4. 看著大綱，完成文章。

The allocation of defence and social benefits in the government budget has caused a large amount [1]**fierce controversy**. It is suggested that the government should spend more on defense to ensure citizens' safety, and meanwhile reduce citizens' social benefits. However, while the safety of a nation is of critical importance, the funding for social welfare [2]**is equally important**.

Undeniably, distributing more money to [3]**strengthen a country's security** is particularly important as it [4]**lays a firm foundation** to a country's stability. Some nations are not on good terms because of territorial or economic issues, but bad relations can [5]**escalates into a full-scale war** [6]**in an instant**. On the contrary, if one country builds powerful military forces, it would [7]**win the respect of** its neighboring countries and thus become the leader of the region. This advantage, in turn, would also result in more [8]**beneficial terms** in international agreements. Another [9]**convincing reason for** increasing defense budget is to [10]**combat international terrorism**. People in any countries, like Iran, have to [11]**face grave threats** and experience terrorist attacks every day. Perhaps only by increasing armed forces can a country reduce threats from terrorists and [12]**nip them in the bud**.

However, the budget on military expansion cannot be [13]**at the expense of** social welfare because the social prosperity is as critical as the military. That is, services like education, medical services, or transportation should also be subsidized too. The government is responsible for ensuring that all the people can [14]**meet their basic needs** such as food, shelter and health as a dearth of social benefits can [15]**inflict a massive damage to** a country's residents. For example, North Korea [16]**strongly emphasizes** the development of military, only to create [17]**a poverty-stricken country**. The country's terrible suffering results from the deficiency of social benefit programs such as retirement schemes, disability benefits and subsidized housing. Worst of all, this can lead to [18]**resentment among the disadvantaged** and [19]**social uprising against the authorities**. However, if offered welfare for the neediest of the society through various plans, the nation can raise their living standards, therefore helping its people become happy and contented.

160

In sum, enforcing the security is extremely crucial for nations to face the enemy nations nearby and terrorism. Nonetheless, social benefits cannot be sacrificed as [20]**a substantial portion of people** are in desperate need of financial support. (387 words)

加分的 Collocations

1. **Adv + Adj** extremely controversial　極具爭議的
 = heated controversy
 = bitter controversy
 = raging controversy
 = violent controversy

2. **Adv + Adj** is equally important　等同重要的
 = is similarly important

3. **Verb + Noun** strengthen a country's security　強化國家安全
 = improve a country's security
 = tighten (up) a country's security

4. **Verb + Adj + Noun** lay a firm foundation for　奠定穩定基礎
 = build a solid foundation for
 = build a sound foundation for
 = build a strong foundation for

5. **Verb + Preposition + Noun** escalate into a full-scale war　演變成全面戰爭
 = turn into a full-sized war

6. **Preposition + Noun** in an instant　立刻
 = in a moment
 = in a flash
 = immediately
 = instantaneously

= instantly

= right away

= right now

= at once

7. **Verb + Noun + Preposition** win the respect of 贏得尊重

= gain the respect of

= get the respect of

= earn the respect of

= command the respect of

8. **Adj + Noun** beneficial terms 有利益的（合約）條件

= favorable contracts

= valuable compacts

= valuable pacts

= valuable deals

9. **Adj + Noun** convincing reason for 有説服力的原因

= compelling reason for

= persuasive reason for

10. **Verb + Noun** combat international terrorism 對抗國際恐怖主義

= fight international terrorism

11. **Verb + Adj + Noun** face grave threats 面對重大威脅

= be faced with considerable threats

= meet considerable threats

= encounter considerable threats

= confront considerable threats

12. **Verb + Noun** nip... in the bud   對⋯⋯防患於未然

= take preventive measures

= take precautionary measures

= take precautions

13. **Preposition + Noun** at the expense of...   以⋯⋯為代價

= at the cost of

14. **Verb + Noun** meet one's basic needs   滿足某人的基本需求

= address their basic needs

= fulfill their basic needs

= satisfy their basic needs

15. **Verb + Noun + Preposition** inflict a massive damage on...   對⋯⋯造成重大傷害

= cause a massive damage to

= do a massive damage to

16. **Adv + Verb** strongly emphasize   非常重視

= put a strong emphasis

= place a great emphasis

= lay a heavy emphasis

17. **Adj + Noun** a poverty-stricken country   貧窮的國家

= a poor country

18. **Noun + Preposition + Noun** resentment among the disadvantaged
                                          貧弱族群的憤恨不滿

= anger among the disadvantaged

= fury among the disadvantaged

19. **Noun + Preposition** social uprising against...　對……的社會反叛

= social rebellion against the authorities

= social revolution against the authorities

= social revolt against the authorities

= social upheaval against the authorities

20. **Adj + Noun** a substantial portion of...　大多數……

= a large number of people

✐ 心得筆記

Day 13　Food

More and more people are becoming seriously overweight. Some people say that raising the price of fast foods will solve this problem.

To what extent do you agree or disagree?

大綱式寫作步驟解析

1. 閱讀題目，劃出分歧（破解題目）：

More and more people are becoming seriously overweight. Some people say that <u>**raising the price of fast foods**</u> will solve this problem.

* **分歧點**：raising the price of fast foods vs. other measures

2. 擬定大綱，確定結構：

第一段 : While **raising the price of fast foods, other measures**

第二段 : **raising the price of fast foods**

第三段 : **other measures**

第四段 : paraphrase your thesis

3. 參考範文／網路文章，找出論點：

2nd paragraph	
Subject:	raising the price of fast foods
Argument:	a rise in the prices of unhealthy food = a great help to avoid eating it
Supporting Ideas:	e.g. adolescents (middle class) eat hamburgers + pizzas in McDonald's, Burger King or KFC ← food there is affordable though give people an appetite junk foods (salty snacks + pizza) are fattening people up ← an excessive amount of sugar, fat, carbohydrates + calories an increase in the price discourage people with a limited budget (1) the price of food ↑ X buy it (2) have healthy, cheap home-made cuisine rather than junk food (3) the percentage of the unfit population ↓

	3rd paragraph
Subject:	other measures
Argument:	an active lifestyle + investment on fitness facilities
Supporting Ideas:	a. w/o an active lifestyle → run the risk of being obese If store too many calories (1) produce adipose tissue in their bodies (2) making them gain too much weight (3) physical activities can help them burn calories + keep fit Research: those (live a sedentary lifestyle) → still become obese if they X keep a nutritional diet b. Gov't build more fitness centres + sports stadiums (1) effectively promotes active, healthy lifestyles + grapple with overweight problems (2) professional trainers give advice on a healthy diet to the general public (3) raise the awareness of + pay attention to healthy, balanced eating habits

4. 看著大綱，完成文章。

Obesity, being [1]**extremely fat** in a way that is dangerous for health, is a major concern in this modern world partly due to [2]**a large intake of** unhealthy foods. However, while some argue it can be put to a stop by [3]**an increment in food prices**, I still believe other measures should [4]**be taken into account** to [5]**totally eliminate obesity**.

Admittedly, not everybody can purchase expensive merchandise and thus a rise in the prices of unhealthy food could become a great help to avoid consuming it. For instance, adolescents, especially the middle class, usually eat hamburgers or pizzas in fast food chains like McDonald's, Burger King or KFC because the food there is affordable. Though the foods [6]**give people an appetite,** it is reported that junk foods are [7]**fattening people up** as they contain an excessive amount of sugar, fat, carbohydrates, and calories. Hence, an increase in the price of this type of food will discourage people with [8]**a limited budget** from buying it and prefer to have healthy, inexpensive [9]**home-made cuisine** rather than junk food; by doing so, [10]**the percentage of the unfit population** would also decrease at the same time.

However, simply raising the price of [11]**calorific foods** cannot effectively address the knotty problem, so other effective tactics should be utilized to help people [12]**lose weight**: an active lifestyle and investment on fitness facilities. Firstly, without an active lifestyle, people are still [13]**run the risk of being obese**. If people store too many calories, they may produce adipose tissue in their bodies, thereby making them [14]**gain too much weight**. Thus, physical activities can help them burn calories and [15]**keep fit**. Recent research concludes that those who just [16]**live a sedentary lifestyle** will still become obese if they do not [17]**keep a nutritional diet**. Secondly, the government can [18]**build more fitness centres and sports stadiums**, which in turn effectively promotes active, healthy lifestyles and grapple with overweight problems. Besides, professional trainers can give advice on a healthy diet to the general public to [19]**raise public awareness of** and pay attention to healthy, balanced eating habits.

In conclusion, an increase in the price of fattening foods can partly solve the problem of obesity, but I think encouraging people to lead an active lifestyle and take exercise can [20]**successfully tackle** the problem. (381 words)

加分的 Collocations

1. | **Adv + Adj** | extremely fat　非常胖
= really fat
= hugely fat
= enormously fat
= immensely fat

2. | **Adj + Noun** | a large intake　大量攝取
= a high consumption of

3. | **Noun + Preposition** | an increment in...　……的增加
= an increase in food prices
= an addition to food prices
= a rise in food prices
= a growth in food prices
= a surge in food prices

4. be taken into account　被考慮到
= be taken into consideration

5. | **Adv + Verb + Noun** | totally eliminate obesity　完全消除肥胖
= altogether eradicate obesity
= completely get rid of obesity

6. | **Verb + Noun** | give sb an appetite　增加某人的食慾
= increase people's appetite

7. **Verb + Noun** fatten sb up　把人養胖

= feed people up

8. **Adj + Noun** a limited budget　有限的預算

= a shoestring budget

= a small budget

= a tight budget

9. **Adj + Noun** home-made cuisine　家常菜

= home-made food

10. **Noun + Preposition + Noun** the percentage of the unfit population

不健康人口的百分比

= the proportion of the unhealthy population

= the number of the unhealthy population

= the figure of the unhealthy population

= the ratio of the unhealthy population

11. **Adj + Noun** calorific foods　高熱量的食物

= calorie-rich foods

= foods high in calories

12. **Verb + Noun** lose weight　減重／肥

= reduce weight

= shed weight

13. **Verb + Noun** run the risk of...　面臨⋯⋯的風險

= face the risk of becoming obese

= take the risk of being fat

14. **Verb + Noun** gain too much weight　變太胖／體重增加過多

= put on excess weight

15. **Verb + Adj** keep fit　保持健康
= stay fit
= be as fit as a fiddle

16. **Verb + Adj + Noun** live a sedentary lifestyle　過著缺少活動的生活
= have an inactive lifestyle
= enjoy a sedentary lifestyle

17. **Verb + Adj + Noun** keep a nutritional diet　保持營養的飲食
= have a calorie-controlled diet
= eat a low-calorie diet
= follow a balanced diet
= stick to a nutritional diet

18. **Verb + Noun** build more fitness centres and sports stadiums
建造更多健身中心以及體育館
= construct more fitness centres and sports stadiums
= develop more fitness centres and sports stadiums
= establish more fitness centres and sports stadiums

19. **Verb + Noun** raise awareness of...　喚醒對於……的意識
= build public awareness of
= develop public awareness of
= encourage public awareness of
= foster public awareness of
= heighten public awareness of
= increase public awareness of

20. **Adv + Verb** successfully tackle　成功解決
= effectively tackle

Day 14   Health

Some people choose to eat no meat or fish. They believe that this not only improves their health but also benefits the world.

Discuss this viewpoint and give your own opinion.

> 大綱式寫作步驟解析

1. 閱讀題目，劃出分歧（破解題目）：

Some people choose to eat no meat or fish. They believe that this not only <u>improves their health</u> but also <u>benefits the world</u>.

* **分歧點**：benefit health + environment vs. not good for everyone

2. 擬定大綱，確定結構：

第一段：While **better for health + environment, not good for everyone**

第二段：**better for health + environment**

第三段：**not good for everyone**

第四段：paraphrase your thesis

3. 參考範文／網路文章，找出論點：

2nd paragraph	
Subject:	benefits of being vegetarians
Argument:	health benefits + environmentally friendly
Supporting Ideas:	a. Studies: vegetarians tend to live longer > their meat eating counterparts ← meat / fish affects the blood tension of those (chronic diseases: diabetes, coronary artery disease, hypertension, obesity, etc.) b. a myriad of animals are raised + slaughtered ← satisfy the demand for meat and fish annually X, livestock → greenhouse gas emissions worldwide If reduce the consumption of meat (1) the need for raising animals decrease (2) the land can be transmuted to grow vegetables (3) produces clean air for the whole world

3rd paragraph	
Subject:	not good for everyone
Argument:	meat and fish are an integral part of a nutritious diet
Supporting Ideas:	Many food scientists: several types of vitamins + proteins from consuming meat + fish e.g., (1) for those in cold countries (X grow vegetables and cereals) → meat consumption = a feasible solution to the inclement weather (2) For those (engage in strenuous physical activities) fish and meat = excellent sources of proteins (3) For those (suffer from cardiovascular diseases) salmon fish → omega-3 fats → beneficial for our blood circulation process (4) For those (suffer from senile dementia) meat = nutrition for the development of human's brain → vegetarianism is not ideal for many of them

4. 看著大綱，完成文章。

[1]**There is no doubt that** there are many health and environmental benefits to vegetarianism. However, while I do agree with this viewpoint, I do not think that vegetarianism is suitable for everyone.

[2]**Adopting a plant-based diet** not only results in some health benefits, but also [3]**improves the environment**. First of all, some studies have shown that vegetarians tend to live longer than their meat eating counterparts because meat or fish affects the [4]**blood tension** of those who suffer from [5]**chronic diseases** such as diabetes, coronary artery disease, hypertension, obesity, etc. Second, [6]**a myriad of** animals are raised and then slaughtered to [7]**satisfy the demand for** meat and fish annually. However, livestock are one of the major causes of greenhouse gas emissions worldwide. If we can reduce the consumption of meat, the need for raising animals will also decrease and [8]**the land used to raise them can be transmuted** to grow vegetables, which thus produces clean air [9]**for the whole world**.

However, being a vegetarian is not an option for everyone because meat and fish are [10]**an integral part of a nutritious diet**. [11]**Many food scientists indicate that** there are several types of vitamins and proteins that can only be acquired from consuming meat and fish. For instance, for those living in cold climates, it is difficult to [12]**grow vegetables and cereals** and hence meat consumption is [13]**a feasible solution** to the [14]**inclement weather**. For those who [15]**engage in strenuous physical activities**, fish and meat are [16]**excellent sources of proteins** for bodybuilders or athletes. For those who suffer from cardiovascular diseases, salmon contains a certain type of oils, like omega-3 fats, which are beneficial for our blood circulation process. For those who suffer from [17]**senile dementia**, meat is essential source of nutrition for [18]**the development of human's brain**. Consequently, vegetarianism is not ideal for everyone.

In conclusion, as previously discussed, being a vegetarian may [19]**have some positive impacts on** our health and the environment, but I believe that skipping fish and meat is not workable for many people, especially when they have certain [20]**health concern**.

(344 words)

加分的 Collocations

1. There is no doubt that... 毫無疑問地／的確如此……
   = Undoubtedly
   = Undeniably
   = Indisputably
   = Unquestionably
   = Admittedly

2. **Verb + Noun** adopt a plant-based diet 選擇素食飲食
   = choose a plant-based diet
   = opt for a plant-based diet

3. **Verb + Noun** damage the environment 破壞環境
   = devastate the environment
   = harm the environment

4. **Noun + Noun** blood tension 高血壓
   = hypertension
   = high blood tension

5. **Adj + Noun** chronic diseases 慢性病
   = long-lasting diseases

6. a myriad of 大量／很多
   = a lot of
   = many
   = a large number of
   = numerous
   = countless
   = innumerable

7. **Verb + Noun** satisfy the demand for...　滿足……的需求
= fulfill the demand for
= meet the demand for

8. **Noun + Verb** the land … can be transmuted　用來…的土地可以變成
= the land … can be transformed
= the land … can be changed
= the land … can be converted

9. **Preposition + Adj + Noun** for the whole world　全世界
= for the entire world

10. **Adj + Noun** an integral part　不可或缺的一部分
= an essential part of
= a necessary part of
= a fundamental part of

11. **Verb + Noun** Many food scientists indicate that　許多食物科學家指出
= Many food scientists point out that
= Many food scientists suggest that
= Many food scientists show that
= Many food scientists reveal that

12. **Verb + Noun** grow vegetables and cereals　栽培蔬菜與麥片
= raise vegetables and cereals
= cultivate vegetables and cereals

13. **Adj + Noun** a feasible solution　可行的解決辦法
= a workable solution
= a practical solution
= a viable solution
= a doable solution

14. **Adj + Noun** inclement weather　惡劣天氣

= bad weather

= appalling weather

= awful weather

= dreadful weather

= gloomy weather

= miserable weather

= rotten weather

= terrible weather

= wretched weather

15. **Verb + Noun** engage in strenuous physical activities　參加激烈運動

= be involved in strenuous physical activities

= participate in strenuous physical activities

= take part in strenuous physical activities

= partake strenuous physical activities

= undertake strenuous physical activities

16. **Adj + Noun** excellent sources of proteins　很棒的蛋白質來源

= reliable sources of proteins

= good sources of proteins

17. **Adj + Noun** senile dementia　老年痴呆症

= Alzheimer's Disease

18. **Noun + Preposition + Noun** the development of human's brain　人腦的發展

= the growth of human's brain

= the advance of human's brain

19. **Verb + Noun** have some positive impacts on　對……有正面影響

= achieve some beneficial impacts on

= create some favorable impacts on

= exert some profound impacts on

= make some substantial impacts on

20. **Noun + Noun** health concern 健康疑慮／擔憂

= health problems

心得筆記

Day 15　Language

Every year several languages die out. Some people think that this is not important because life will be easier if there are fewer languages in the world.

To what extent do you agree or disagree with this opinion?

大綱式寫作步驟解析

1. 閱讀題目，劃出分歧（破解題目）：

Every year several languages die out. Some people think that this is not important because **life will be easier** if there are fewer languages in the world.

  * **分歧點**：life will be easier vs. life will not be easier

2. 擬定大綱，確定結構：

第一段 : While **life will be easier, life will not be easier**

第二段 : **life will be easier**

第三段 : **life will not be easier**

第四段 : paraphrase your thesis

3. 參考範文／網路文章，找出論點：

2nd paragraph	
Subject:	life will be easier
Argument:	economy + travel
Supporting Ideas:	a. Economically: English = global lingua franca facilitates cross-cultural communication + enhances efficacy → various multinational companies are devising strategies to communicate in English Communication in English (1) minimize potential problems arise due to lack of communication (2) further bring about better work performance b. From the perspective of travel: language barriers + communicative impediments might be greatly reduced → when visiting other countries, people speak with the locals easily ← they share the same language

3rd paragraph	
Subject:	life will be not easier
Argument:	cultural diversity + a nation's economy
Supporting Ideas:	a. Culturally: the obliteration of the languages in danger = extinction of its cultures ← each language is closely entwined with cultures unique culture → make a country worth being visited X, a loss in languages would put an end to the long-established lifestyles of people b. From the perspective of economy: if non-English-speaking countries stop speaking their first languages + start using English instead → their lifestyles also change radically + become analogous to those of the American If this happens → lose its appeal as a tourist destination ← the dearth of cultural distinctions + diversities

4. 看著大綱，完成文章。

Recently, [1]**the number of** the languages around the world has been diminishing every year. Many people consider it is a positive development because life will become easier if [2]**several languages die out**. However, while extinction of languages may bring about positive results to our life, I think this trend will do harm to individuals and the society as a whole.

On the one hand, if people speak fewer languages, life can be easier in several aspects. Economically, English as a global lingua franca facilitates [3]**cross-cultural communication** and [4]**enhances efficacy**, so various multinational companies [5]**are devising strategies** for their employees to communicate in English. Communication in English will [6]**minimize potential problems** that may arise due to lack of communication and further bring about better work performance. From the perspective of travel, [7]**language barriers** and [8]**ineffective communication** might be greatly reduced. Thus, when visiting other countries, people would interact successfully with the locals easily because they can share the same language.

On the other hand, language extinctions can lead to [9]**a detrimental impact on** cultural diversity and a nation's economy. Culturally, [10]**the obliteration of the languages** means extinction of its cultures because each language [11]**is closely entwined with** cultures. After all, it is the unique culture that makes a country worth being visited. On the contrary, a loss in languages will probably [12]**put an end to** the [13]**long-established lifestyles** of people who speak those languages. Furthermore, [14]**as far as the economy is concerned**, if some non-English-speaking countries suddenly stop speaking their first languages and start using English instead, their lifestyles will also [15]**change radically** and [16]**become analogous to** those of the American. If this happens, a region will lose its appeal as [17]**a tourist destination** owing to [18]**the dearth of** cultural distinctions and diversities.

In conclusion, even though people have [19]**a divergent view on** whether the language extinction causes any problem, I do believe that this will [20]**be deleterious to** individuals and the whole society. (324 words)

1. **Noun + Verb** the number of... has been diminishing……　的數量不斷減少
   = the number of … has been decreasing
   = the number of … has been declining
   = the number of … has been reducing
   = the number of … has been dropping
   = the number of … has been falling

2. **Noun + Verb** several languages die out　一些語言消失
   = several languages die off
   = several languages vanish
   = several languages perish
   = several languages disappear

3. **Adj + Noun** cross-cultural communication　跨文化溝通／交流
   = cross-cultural interaction

4. **Verb + Noun** enhance efficacy　提升效率
   = improve effectiveness
   = increase effectiveness
   = maximize effectiveness

5. **Verb + Noun** devise strategies　制定策略
   = design strategies
   = develop strategies
   = formulate strategies
   = map out strategies
   = plan strategies
   = work out strategies

6. **Verb + Adj + Noun** minimize potential problems　將可能發生的問題降到最低
= decrease possible problems
= reduce possible problems

7. **Noun + Noun** language barriers　語言隔閡
= linguistic barriers
= communication barriers
= communication impediment
= communication difficulties

8. **Adj + Noun** ineffective communication　無效的溝通交流
= poor communication

9. **Adj + Noun + Preposition** a detrimental impact on　負面衝擊
= an adverse impact on
= a catastrophic impact on
= a damaging impact on
= a devastating impact on
= a disastrous impact on
= a heavy impact on
= a negative impact on

10. **Noun + Preposition + Noun** the obliteration of languages　語言的滅絕
= the destruction of the languages
= the annihilation of the languages
= the eradication of the languages
= the elimination of the languages
= the loss of languages
= the disappearance of languages
= the extermination of languages
= the extinction of languages

11. **Adv + Adj** be closely entwined with...　與……關係相當緊密

= be closely connected with

= be intimately related to

= be strongly correlated with

= be directly linked to

= be strongly associated with

12. **Verb + Noun + Preposition** put an end to...　終結……

= put a stop to

= bring to an end

= terminate

= end

13. **Adj + Noun** long-established lifestyles　建立以久的生活型態

= long-lasting lifestyles

= deep-rooted lifestyles

= engrained/ingrained lifestyles

14. as far as sth is concerned　就……而言

= from the perspective of the economy

= from the angle of the economy

= in terms of the economy

15. **Verb + Adv** change radically　大幅度地改變

= change significantly

= change considerably

= change drastically

= change dramatically

= change substantially

= change fundamentally

16. **Verb + Adj + Preposition** become analogous to　變成類似

= be similar to

= be comparable to

= resemble

17. **Noun + Noun** a tourist destination　旅遊景點

= a beauty spot

= a scenic spot

18. a dearth of...　缺少……

= the lack of

= the shortage of

19. **Adj + Noun** a divergent view on...　對……有不同的看法

= a differing view on

= an opposing view on

= a polarized view on

20. be deleterious to...　對……有害的

= be harmful to

= be damaging to

= be detrimental to

= be injurious to

Day 16　Reading

Some people think that children who spend a lot of time reading storybooks are wasting their time which could be better used doing other more useful activities.

To what extent do you agree or disagree?

大綱式寫作步驟解析

1. 閱讀題目，劃出分歧（破解題目）：

... spend a lot of time **reading storybooks** are wasting their time which could be better used **doing other more useful activities**.

* **分歧點**：reading storybooks vs. other more useful activities

2. 擬定大綱，確定結構：

第一段 : While **reading storybooks, other more useful activities**

第二段 : **reading storybooks**

第三段 : **other more useful activities**

第四段 : paraphrase your thesis

3. 參考範文／網路文章，找出論點：

2nd paragraph	
Subject:	reading storybooks
Argument:	children's physical + mental health
Supporting Ideas:	a. Physically: reading strengthens their brains ← involves a complex network of circuits + signals in the brain As reading ability matures → those networks get stronger + more sophisticated If begin in early childhood + continue through the senior years → benefits last a long time b. Mentally: storybooks are imperative ← an opportunity to learn basic lessons of life (respect for the elderly in a natural way by using visual aids like pictures, paintings, + cartoons) these storybooks sharpen children's analytical skills ← they are taken into a new world → nurtures their brain to develop ideas for new worlds + other possibilities → thereby firing their imagination

3rd paragraph	
Subject:	other more useful activities
Argument:	complete development + emotional bond
Supporting Ideas:	a. engage in physical activities 　←　gain social skills for their complete development = a 　　　crucial part of functioning in society e.g., when they dance, paint or do a jigsaw puzzle → a chance to immerse themselves in the real world unlike stories where a child stays in the imaginary world Through diverse activities → learn many key collaborative skills (1) negotiation (2) coordination (3) planning (4) communication abilities b. spend quality time with their family (1) playing a board game (2) gardening (3) playing outdoors → greater emotional bond within families ←　is of vital importance for children's learning + 　　socialization

4. 看著大綱，完成文章。

Many people think that reading storybooks is [1]**a waste of time** because childhood is the formative period of life to [2]**construct their learning**. While I accept that children should spend some time reading fascinating stories, I do believe that they should also [3]**be actively involved in** other productive activities.

First and foremost, storybooks [4]**occupy a vital role in** children's physical and mental health. Physically, reading [5]**strengthens their brains** because reading involves [6]**a complex network of circuits and signals** in the brain. As their reading ability matures, those networks also get stronger and more sophisticated. If they begin reading in early childhood and continue through the senior years, these benefits can last for a long time. Mentally, storybooks are imperative as they are furnished with an opportunity to learn basic lessons of life, such as respect for the elderly, in a natural way by using visual aids like pictures, paintings, and cartoons. Furthermore, these storybooks can also help [7]**sharpen children's analytical skills**. While reading, they are taken into a new world, which nurtures their brain to develop ideas and other possibilities, thereby [8]**firing their imagination**.

However, the same time can also be utilized to participate in other equally or more important activities. First, children should [9]**engage in various activities** to gain social skills, which is a crucial part of [10]**functioning in society**. For example, when they dance, paint or [11]**do a jigsaw puzzle**, they are given a chance to [12]**immerse themselves in** the real world, unlike stories where a child stays [13]**in the imaginary world**. Through diverse activities, children can learn many key collaborative skills, including negotiation, coordination, and communication abilities, and even [14]**build friendship**. Second, [15]**apart from reading storybooks**, they have to [16]**spend quality time with their family**. Spending time in everyday family leisure activities, such as playing a board game, gardening or playing outdoors, is proved to be associated with greater [17]**emotional bond** within families, which is [18]**of vital importance** for children's learning and socialization.

In conclusion, although storybooks [19]**have a far-reaching impact on** children's physical and mental development, I believe children should also spare some time for other activities to both polish their social skills and [20]**build family closeness**. (361 words)

1. a waste of time　浪費時間

2. **Verb + Noun** construct their learning　建構學習
   = develop their learning
   = cultivate their learning
   = nurture their learning
   = foster their learning

3. **Adv + Adj** be actively involved in...　積極參與……
   = actively participate in
   = fully partake in
   = actively take part in

4. **Verb + Noun** occupy a vital role　扮演很重要的角色
   = play a crucial role in
   = perform a pivotal role in
   = take an essential role in

5. **Verb + Noun** strengthen sb's brains　強化腦力
   = boost their brainpower

6. **Adj + Noun** a complex network of circuits and signals　複雜的迴路與訊號的網路
   = a complicated network of circuits and signals
   = an elaborate network of circuits and signals
   = an intricate network of circuits and signals
   = an intensive network of circuits and signals

7. **Verb + Noun** sharpen children's analytical skills　改善小孩的分析能力
= improve children's analytical skills
= increase children's analytical skills
= polish children's analytical skills
= broaden children's analytical skills
= hone children's analytical skills
= master children's analytical skills
= upgrade children's analytical skills

8. **Verb + Noun** fire their imagination　激發想像力
= stir their imagination
= stimulate their imagination
= inspire their imagination

9. **Verb + Noun** engage in various activities　做很多不同的運動
= be involved in various activities
= take part in various activities
= participate in various activities
= partake in various activities

10. function in society　在社會正常生活

11. **Verb + Noun** do a jigsaw puzzle　玩拼圖
= piece together a jigsaw puzzle

12. **Verb + Noun + Preposition** immerse oneself in the real world　沈浸在真實世界中
= revel in the real world

13. **Adj + Noun** in the imaginary world　在想像的世界
= in the fantasy world
= in the made-up world
= in the invented world
= in the fictional world

14. **Verb + Noun** build friendship　建立友誼

= establish friendship

= form friendship

15. **Preposition + Noun** apart from reading storybooks　除了閱讀故事書

= in addition to reading storybooks

16. **Verb + Noun** spend quality time with their family　花時間跟家人相處

= spend precious time with their family

17. **Adj + Noun** emotional bond　情感的連結

= emotional connection

= emotional tie

= emotional link

= emotional attachment

18. **Preposition + Adj + Noun** of vital importance　非常重要的

= of critical importance

= of crucial importance

= of profound importance

= of supreme importance

= of supreme importance

= of paramount importance

19. **Verb + Noun + Preposition** have a far-reaching impact on　有很深遠的影響

= achieve a wider impact on

= create a favorable impact on

= exert a profound impact on

= make a substantial impact on

20. **Verb + Noun** build family closeness　建立家庭親密關係

= establish family closeness

= form family closeness

= develop family closeness

= foster family closeness

✏️ 心得筆記

Day 17　Transport

In the future all cars, buses and trucks will be driverless. The only people travelling inside these vehicles will be passengers.

Do you think the advantages of driverless vehicles outweigh the disadvantages?

(大綱式寫作步驟解析)

1. 閱讀題目，劃出分歧（破解題目）：

Do you think the **advantages** of driverless vehicles outweigh the **disadvantages**?

* 分歧點：advantages vs. disadvantages

2. 擬定大綱，確定結構：

第一段：While **advantages, disadvantages**

第二段：**advantages**

第三段：**disadvantages**

第四段：paraphrase your thesis

3. 參考範文／網路文章，找出論點：

2nd paragraph	
Subject:	advantages
Argument:	safety + reduction of corporate operation expenses
Supporting Ideas:	a. proponents of this technology: driverless vehicles cause fewer accidents than human-driven ones ← humans are prone to errors (1) fatigue (2) distractions from smartphones (3) drunk driving (4) speeding Machines have technical glitches, X in fact, probability of accidents ↓ ⇔ if driverless → eliminate automobile accidents b. businesses X hire drivers to distribute their products or services e.g., a Taiwanese logistics company (HCT Logistics) pay each of them an average of NT450,000 dollars = billions of dollars annually Substituting automated vehicles for these drivers → colossal salary payments be significantly reduced

3rd paragraph	
Subject:	disadvantages
Argument:	safety + moral dilemma + loss of jobs + high maintenance costs
Supporting Ideas:	a. safety: driverless vehicles rely on state-of-the-art technology for its operation any accident ← hacking or malfunctioning → collisions + the loss of precious lives but machines X be wholly responsible for the potential loss b. moral dilemma: lack of ability to make judgments between multiple unfavorable outcomes e.g., face the moral dilemma of whether veers (1) to the left + strikes a pedestrian or (2) to the right, hits a tree, potentially injuring passengers c. loss of jobs: (1) truckers (2) Uber drivers (3) bus drivers (4) delivery couriers → a rise of unemployment d. high maintenance costs + yearly check-ups ← ensure safe operation

4. 看著大綱，完成文章。

高分範文

A future filled with driverless vehicles [1]**seems apparently inevitable**. However, in my opinion, the disadvantages of driverless vehicles outweigh its advantages.

Admittedly, [2]**automated vehicles** can give rise to two advantages: safety and reduction of corporate operation expenses. Firstly, [3]**proponents of this technology claim that** driverless vehicles cause fewer accidents than human-driven ones because humans [4]**are prone to errors** due to fatigue, distractions from smartphones, drunk driving, and speeding. Machines might have [5]**technical glitches** occasionally, but in fact, the probability of accidents seems to be lower. That is, if all cars were driverless, this would [6]**eliminate automobile accidents**. Secondly, with these driverless cars, businesses would not need to hire drivers to [7]**distribute their products or services** to their customers. For example, a Taiwanese logistics company, HCT Logistics with hundreds of truck drivers, has to pay each of them an average of NT450,000 dollars every year, which [8]**totals billions of dollars** annually. [9]**Substituting** automated vehicles **for these drivers** means that these [10]**colossal salary payments** could be significantly reduced.

Nevertheless, the disadvantages caused by self-driving cars may lead to four [11]**grave consequences**. In terms of safety, driverless vehicles [12]**rely heavily on** [13]**state-of-the-art technology** for its operation. Any accident that happens because of hacking or malfunctioning will cause collisions and even the loss of precious lives, but unfortunately machines cannot [14]**be wholly responsible for** the loss. Another downside is their lack of ability to [15]**make judgments** between multiple unfavorable outcomes. For instance, a self-driving car may [16]**face the moral dilemma of** whether it veers to the left and [17]**strikes a pedestrian** or to the right, hits a tree, potentially injuring passengers inside the vehicle. Third, driverless vehicles would cause loss of jobs for drivers, such as truckers, Uber drivers, bus drivers, or delivery couriers, thus resulting in a rise of unemployment. Finally, driverless vehicles would require high [18]**maintenance costs** and [19]**yearly check-ups** to ensure safe operation.

In conclusion, driverless vehicles would bring positive effects, but there are many potential drawbacks that need to be overcome before this technology becomes [20]**completely safe** for everyone. (339 words)

加分的 Collocations

1. **Verb + Adv + Adj** seem apparently inevitable 似乎是無法避免的
= appear seemingly predictable
= look seemingly unavoidable

2. **Adj + Noun** automated vehicles 自動駕駛汽車
= automatic vehicles
= autonomous vehicles
= self-driving vehicles
= robotic vehicles

3. **Noun + Verb** proponents of this technology claim that 這項科技提倡者認為
= proponents of this technology argue that
= proponents of this technology contend that
= proponents of this technology believe that
= proponents of this technology think that
= proponents of this technology assert that
= proponents of this technology maintain that

4. **Verb + Adj + Preposition** are prone to errors 容易出錯
= be susceptible to errors
= be vulnerable to errors
= be liable to errors
= be subject to errors
= be predisposed to errors

5. **Adj + Noun** technical glitches 故障
= mechanical failure

6. **Verb + Noun** eliminate automobile accidents　減少車禍
= reduce automobile accidents

7. **Verb + Noun** distribute their products or services　配送產品或服務
= deliver their goods or services
= transport their commodities or services
= send their merchandise or services

8. **Verb + Noun** total billions of dollars　總金額是好幾十億以上
= add up to billions of dollars
= equal billions of dollars
= amount to billions of dollars
= tot up billions of dollars

9. **Verb + Noun** substitute automated vehicles for these drivers
　　　　　　　用自動駕駛取代這些司機
= replace these drivers with automated vehicles
= supersede these drivers with automated vehicles

注意：substitute 和另外 replace/supersede 的用法不一樣。
substitute A for B，表示「用 A 來取代 B」。
= replace B with A
= supersede B with A

10. **Adj + Noun** colossal salary payments　巨大薪資支付
= huge salary payments
= massive salary payments
= enormous salary payments
= vast salary payments
= substantial salary payments

11. **Adj + Noun** grave consequence　嚴重後果

= dire consequences

= adverse consequences

= damaging consequences

= serious consequences

= severe consequences

= devastating consequences

= disastrous consequences

= terrible consequences

= tragic consequences

12. **Verb + Adv + Preposition** rely heavily on　非常依靠

= depend greatly on

= rest heavily on

= bank heavily on

= count heavily on

= hinge strongly on

13. **Adj + Noun** state-of-the-art technology　最新科技

= leading-edge technology

= advanced technology

= high technology

= sophisticated technology

= up-to-date technology

14. **Adv + Adj** be wholly responsible for　完全負責

= be entirely responsible for

= be totally responsible for

15. **Verb + Noun** make judgments　做出判斷

= form judgments

16. **Verb + Noun** face the moral dilemma of　面對道德上的兩難

= be caught in the moral quandary of

= be faced with the moral predicament of

= confront the moral dilemma of

= be in the pretty pickle

17. **Verb + Noun** strike a pedestrian　衝撞行人

= hit a pedestrian

= collide with a pedestrian

= run into a pedestrian

18. **Noun + Noun** maintenance costs　維修成本

= running costs

= running outlay

= running expenses

= running expenditure

19. **Adj + Noun** yearly check-ups　每年定期檢查

= annual examination

= annual inspection

20. **Adv + adj** completely safe　相當安全

= perfectly safe

= totally safe

Day 18 Travel

International tourism has brought enormous benefits to many places. At the same time, there is concern about its impact on local inhabitants and the environment.

Do the disadvantages of international tourism outweigh the advantages?

大綱式寫作步驟解析

1. 閱讀題目，劃出分歧（破解題目）：

International tourism has brought enormous **benefit** to many places. Meanwhile, there is **concern** about its impact on local inhabitants and the environment.

* 分歧點：benefits vs. concern

2. 擬定大綱，確定結構：

第一段 : While **concern**, **benefits**

第二段 : **concern**

第三段 : **benefits**

第四段 : paraphrase your thesis

3. 參考範文／網路文章，找出論點：

2nd paragraph	
Subject:	concern
Argument:	negative ramifications on locals + the environment
Supporting Ideas:	a. for inhabitants: tourism may pose a threat to their lives ← a rise in travelers = an increase in air, noise, and water pollution Also, a flood of holidaymakers = increasing rates of crimes, prostitution + antisocial activities (drugs, smuggling, human trafficking + gambling) b. for environments more low-cost flights → excessive emission of CO_2 trees are felled every day ← build resorts + hotels to accommodate tourists heavy littering wastage → puts an incredible strain on local waste management systems

	3rd paragraph
Subject:	benefits
Argument:	economic + cultural impacts
Supporting Ideas:	a. Economically: jobs from a huge influx of visitors (1) not only generate a number of job opportunities (2) but boost the economy as well ← the money makes up a significant proportion in private, local, + national incomes e.g., visitors spend money (1) staying at hotels (2) eating at restaurants (3) using taxis → ↑ revenue for business owners involved in these industries → ↑ the standard of living for the local community b. Culturally: gain immeasurable benefits from exposing themselves to a new culture (new cuisine + traditional garments) → promotes their international connections + broadens their thinking (1) foster cultural collaborations (2) raise cross-cultural awareness (3) build bridges of understanding between cultures for the local communities

4. 看著大綱，完成文章。

Nowadays, tourism industry has [1]**created a boom** for several places by not only [2]**yielding substantial revenue** but also offering employment opportunities. However, while there are some possible shortcomings of international tourism, especially the negative influence on local inhabitants and the environment, I deeply believe that the merits of tourism [3]**surpass its demerits**.

Undoubtedly, travels between countries [4]**have negative ramifications on** locals and the environment. First and foremost, for inhabitants, tourism may pose a threat to their lives because a rise in travelers means an increase in air, noise, and water pollution in the local area. Also, [5]**a flood of holidaymakers** are linked with increasing rates of crimes, prostitution and antisocial activities like drugs, smuggling, human trafficking and gambling. Secondly, international tourism impacts the environment considerably. For example, more and more travelers choose [6]**low-cost flights**, which leads to excessive emission of CO_2. In addition, trees are felled every day in order to build resorts and hotels to accommodate a large number of tourists. On top of that, [7]**heavy littering wastage** [8]**puts an incredible strain on** local waste management systems.

Despite these [9]**serious repercussions**, tourism has economic and cultural impacts on the tourist spots. Economically, jobs generated from [10]**a huge influx of visitors** not only help generate a number of job opportunities but [11]**boost the economy** as well because the money [12]**makes up a significant proportion in** private, local, and national incomes. For example, visitors have to spend money staying at hotels, eating at restaurants, and using taxis, which will increase revenue for business owners involved in these industries and thus [13]**raise the standard of living** for the local community. Culturally, while traveling, tourists may [14]**gain immeasurable benefits** from [15]**exposing themselves to a new culture**, such as new cuisine and traditional garments, which in turn [16]**promotes their international connections** and [17]**broadens their thinking**. In addition to the advantages to tourists, tourism can also [18]**foster cultural collaborations**, [19]**raise cross-cultural awareness**, and [20]**build bridges of understanding between cultures for the local communities**.

To sum up, international tourism gives rise to advantages and disadvantages, but the economic and cultural benefits overshadow its demerits. (348 words)

1. **Verb + Noun** create a boom 創造繁榮
= create prosperity
= create growth
= create development

2. **Verb + Noun** yield substantial revenue　產生可觀的收入
= produce considerable revenue
= generate considerable revenue
= bring considerable revenue

3. **Verb + Noun** surpass its demerits　勝過它的缺點
= outperform its demerits
= outshine its demerits
= outdo its demerits
= better its demerits
= overshadow its demerits

4. **Verb + Noun + Preposition** have negative ramifications on　有負面的影響
= have harmful effects on
= have damaging impacts on
= have deleterious influences on
= have destructive effects on
= have adverse effects on

5. a flood of holidaymakers　大量旅客
= a lot of travelers
= a host of visitors
= a large number of tourists
= countless vacationers
= loads of sightseers
= scores of trippers

6. **Adj + Noun** low-cost flights　廉價航空
= budget airlines

7. **Adj + Noun** heavy littering wastage　大量垃圾消耗
= high littering waste
= excessive littering waste

8. **Verb + Adj + Noun + Preposition** put an incredible strain on...
　對……造成極大負擔
= place a heavy burden on

9. **Adj + Noun** serious repercussions　嚴重的後果
= dire consequences
= bad effects
= negative outcomes
= catastrophic impacts

10. a huge influx of visitors　大量旅客湧入
= a vast influx of visitors
= a large influx of visitors

11. **Verb + Noun** boost the economy　提振經濟
= develop the economy
= expand the economy
= kick-start the economy
= reinvigorate the economy
= revive the economy
= stimulate the economy
= strengthen the economy

12. **Verb + Noun** make up a significant proportion　佔據大量部分
= account for a large proportion in
= constitute an overwhelming proportion in
= comprise a huge proportion in

13. **Verb + Noun** raise the standard of living　提升生活水準

= improve the standard of living

14. **Verb + Noun** gain invaluable experience　獲得寶貴經驗

= obtain vast benefits

= get massive benefits

= gain colossal benefits

15. **Verb + Noun + Preposition** expose oneself to...　有機會體驗……

= get exposure to a new culture

= have exposure to a new culture

16. **Verb + Noun** promote their international connections　與國際接軌

= establish their international connections

17. **Verb + Noun** broaden one's thinking　拓展思維

= develop their thinking

= widen their horizons

= expand their horizons

18. **Verb + Noun** foster cultural collaborations　促進文化合作

= promote cultural collaborations

= advance cultural collaborations

= cultivate cultural collaborations

= further cultural collaborations

= develop cultural collaborations

19. **Verb + Noun** raise cross-cultural awareness　提升跨文化的意識

= promote cross-cultural awareness

20. **Verb + Noun** build bridges of understanding　建立互相理解的橋樑

= bridge the gap between cultures for the local communities

Day 19 Society

In many countries women no longer feel the need to get married. Some people believe that this is because women are able to earn their own income and therefore do not require the financial secutiry that marriage can bring.

To what extent do you agree or disagree?

（大綱式寫作步驟解析）

1. 閱讀題目，劃出分歧（破解題目）：

In many countries women no longer feel the need to **get married**. Some people believe that this is because women are able to **earn their own income** and therefore **do not require the financial security** that marriage can bring.

* **分歧點**：agree vs. other reasons

2. 擬定大綱，確定結構：

第一段 : While **agree, other reasons**

第二段 : **agree**

第三段 : **other reasons**

第四段 : paraphrase your thesis

3. 參考範文／網路文章，找出論點：

2nd paragraph	
Subject:	agree
Argument:	being able to earn adequate money = gain secure income source
Supporting Ideas:	a. X traditional values in the past: financially dependent + socially inferior nowadays, both economic + social situations have changed ← hired in various positions that earn sufficient money to cover their living expenditure This economic independence + stability (1) hike up social dignity (2) embrace independence (3) stay away from marriage (devote a greater responsibility + commitment b. females are entitled to claim superannuation from companies + governments = a sum of money for those who reach the retirement age → have a self-reliant elderly life This money → more financial security > any marriage

3rd paragraph	
Subject:	other reasons why women choose not to get married
Argument:	loss of freedom + changes in attitude toward marriage
Supporting Ideas:	a. getting married = the harbinger of loss of freedom: 　Before marriage, girls X restricted to go outside / do 　anything 　X, after marriage 　(1) follow the ethical norms 　(2) accept the values 　(3) fulfill the duties 　(4) even adopt upbringing of in-laws-family b. attitude toward marriage: 　for women (achieve some success in their life) 　getting married = the stumbling block to achievement 　← marriage will divert their attention away from work 　marriage is based largely on 　(1) understanding 　(2) respect 　(3) trust 　(4) X gaining financial security 　Before tie the knot, the one can 　(1) help them dispel the fear of divorce + the instability 　　of marriage 　(2) offer the foundation to weather life's storms

4. 看著大綱，完成文章。

It is argued that the need for matrimony is not emphasized in several nations nowadays as individuals [1]**are financially dependent** and no longer [2]**regard** marriage **as** [3]**a means of financial security**. While I have to admit it is some true [4]**to some extent**, there are also other reasons involved in this changing trend.

Of course, being able to earn adequate money helps women to gain secure income source without spouses' support. Unlike traditional values in the past when most women were financially dependent and [5]**socially inferior**, nowadays, both the economic and social situations have changed because women are hired in various positions that earn sufficient money to [6]**cover their living expenditure**. This [7]**economic independence and stability** may further [8]**hike up their social dignity** and help them [9]**embrace independence**, so they want to [10]**stay away from marriage**, where they have to [11]**devote a greater responsibility and commitment**. Furthermore, females are entitled to claim superannuation from companies and governments, a sum of money for those who reach the retirement age, so they can have [12]**a self-reliant elderly life**. This money provides more financial security than any marriage does.

However, there are other reasons why women choose not to get married—loss of freedom and changes in attitude toward marriage. First of all, getting married is [13]**the harbinger of loss of freedom**. Before marriage, girls are not restricted to go outside their home or do anything they want. However, after marriage, married women have to follow the [14]**ethical norms,** accept the values, fulfill the duties, and even [15]**adopt upbringing of in-law family**. Second, attitude toward marriage has changed especially for women who want to [16]**achieve some success** in their life. Getting married for them becomes [17]**the stumbling block to achievement** since marriage will [18]**divert their attention away from** work. For many women, marriage is based largely on understanding, respect, and trust, rather than just gaining financial security. Before they decide to [19]**tie the knot**, they have to assure the one who can help them dispel the fear of divorce and the instability of marriage and offer the foundation to [20]**weather life's storms**.

In conclusion, many women eschew marriage partly because they are financially independent and do not need the economic security, but I think freedom loss and attitude changes are the main reasons behind this phenomenon. (383 words)

加分的 Collocations

1. **Adv + Adj** are financially dependent　財務依賴
= are economically dependent
= are fiscally dependent
= are monetarily dependent

2. **Verb + Noun + Preposition** regard A as B　把 A 視為 B
= deem marriage as
= consider marriage as
= view marriage as

3. a means of...　……的手段／方法
= a way of economic security
= a method of fiscal security

4. **Preposition + Noun** to some extent　某種程度上
= to some degree

5. **Adv + Adj** socially inferior　社會上弱勢／地位低
= socially minor

6. **Verb + Noun** cover their living expenditure　支付他們生活的開銷
= afford their living expenditure
= pay their living expense

7. **Adj + Noun** economic independence and stability　經濟獨立與穩定

8. **Verb + Noun** hike up their social dignity　提升她們社會尊嚴
= enhance their social dignity

9. **Verb + Noun** embrace independence　接受獨立
= accept independence
= adopt independence
= welcome independence

10. **Verb + Noun** stay away from...　遠離……
= keep away from marriage
= stave off marriage
= ward off marriage
= fend off marriage

11. **Verb + Noun** devote a greater responsibility and commitment　付出責任與奉獻
= dedicate a greater responsibility and promise

12. **Adj + Noun** a self-reliant elderly life　自給自足的老年生活
= a self-sufficient elderly life
= a self-contained elderly life

13. **Noun + Preposition + Noun** the harbinger of loss of freedom　象徵自由的失去
= the indication of loss of freedom
= the sign of loss of freedom
= the omen of loss of freedom
= the portent of loss of freedom
= the precursor of loss of freedom
= the forerunner of loss of freedom
= the herald of loss of freedom

14. **Adj + Noun** ethical norms　道德規範

= ethical standards

= ethical customs

= moral rules

15. **Verb + Noun** adopt upbringing of in-law family　採取夫家的教養方式

= accept education of in-law family

= embrace rearing of in-law family

= take nurture of in-law family

16. **Verb + Noun** achieve some success　成功

= attain some success

= have some success

= notch up some success

= enjoy some success

17. **Noun + Preposition + Noun** the stumbling block to achievement　成功的絆腳石

= the obstacle to achievement

18. **Verb + Noun + Preposition** divert (one's) attention away from...　分散對……的注意

= distract their attention away from⋯

19. **Verb + Noun** tie the knot　結婚

= walk down the aisle

= get hitched

20. **Verb + Noun** weather life's storms　度過生活中的風暴

= ride out life's storms

Day 20　Sport

Some people think that sport teaches children how to compete, while others believe that children learn teamwork.

Discuss both views and give your opinion.

（ 大綱式寫作步驟解析 ）

1. 閱讀題目，劃出分歧（破解題目）：

Some people think that sport teaches children how to **compete**, while others believe that children learn **teamwork**.

* 分歧點：compete vs. teamwork

2. 擬定大綱，確定結構：

第一段：While **compete, teamwork**

第二段：**compete**

第三段：**teamwork**

第四段：paraphrase your thesis

3. 參考範文／網路文章，找出論點：

2nd paragraph	
Subject:	compete
Argument:	do their utmost + finally stand out in the crowd

Supporting Ideas:	sports entail a fierce competition
	    ← a sports event is aimed at determining
	    (1) the best
	    (2) the strongest
	    (3) the fastest
	
	teach how to compete + even outshine others
	    → inculcate the spirit of diligence, endeavor, +
	       persistence
	
	For those (wish to win the competition):
	apply themselves to making the cut
	    → the feeling to outperform others arises spontaneously
	
	e.g., in prestigious colleges (Oxford or UCL)
	the criteria of admission are based on a range of grades
	
	students (highest marks) get their names on the merit list
	+ be admitted
	
	Through the process, learn the essence of competition
	(1) not only have to put in a great deal of effort
	(2) but also push themselves to the limit to outshine their
	    rivals

3rd paragraph	
Subject:	teamwork
Argument:	emphasize teamwork + foster creativity

Supporting Ideas:	a. demonstrate increased cooperation + teamwork
	  → cultivate a sense of community
	  ← a sense of shared responsibility for the upshot
	  → the key to success as a team lies in teamwork, X an individual's talent
	
	teammates learn to support each other through up + down
	
	mutual cooperation + better coordination
	  → clinch well-deserved victory even during a losing streak
	
	b. stimulates students' creativity that solitary work usually lacks
	brainstorming ideas as a team
	(1) helps them brainstorm ways
	(2) elevate their performance > effective than working alone
	
	if teachers inculcate the nature of teamwork in the students
	(1) this infusion can be advantageous
	(2) will give them higher chances to succeed

4. 看著大綱，完成文章。

Sports function as great opportunities for teaching children sportsmanship. While I accept that sports encourage the young to compete with others, I deeply believe they can also learn to work as a team.

Undeniably, competitive nature encourages children to [1]**do their utmost** and finally [2]**stand out** in the crowd. In other words, sports [3]**entail a fierce competition** in every field because a sports event [4]**is aimed at** determining the best, the strongest or the fastest athletes. Teaching children how to compete and even [5]**outshine others** can [6]**inculcate the spirit of** diligence, endeavor, and persistence **in** the children. For those who desire to win the competition, they have to [7]**apply themselves** to [8]**making the cut** and hence [9]**the feeling to outperform others arises** spontaneously. For instance, in [10]**prestigious colleges**, like Oxford or UCL, the criteria of admission are based on a range of grades. Students with highest marks can [11]**get their names on the merit list** and [12]**be admitted into these colleges**. Through the process, they learn the essence of competition. They not only have to put in a great deal of effort but also [13]**push themselves to the limit** to outshine their rivals.

However, children can also learn teamwork and [14]**foster creativity** in a sport competition. First, those who play team sports demonstrate increased cooperation and teamwork and even [15]**cultivate a sense of community** because there is [16]**a sense of shared responsibility** for the upshot, meaning that the key to success as a team lies in teamwork rather than an individual's talent. During the competition, teammates learn to support each other through up and down, and mutual cooperation and better coordination among the team members can even help them [17]**clinch well-deserved victory** even during a losing streak. Second, sports teamwork stimulates students' creativity that solitary work usually lacks when they work together as a team. Brainstorming ideas as a team helps them [18]**brainstorm ways** to [19]**elevate their performance**, which is more effective than working alone. Thus, if teachers can inculcate the nature of teamwork in the students, this infusion can be advantageous for them and will give them higher chances to succeed in various parts of life.

In conclusion, competition and teamwork are two essential qualities which can be learned from competition. These qualities can help children [20]**unlock their potential**, develop creativity, and achieve their goals. (386 words)

> **加分的 Collocations**

1. **Verb + Noun** do their utmost　盡全力
   = try the utmost
   = do their best
   = try their best

2. **Noun + Verb** sb stand out　出類拔萃
   = sb be distinguished
   = sb be pre-eminent
   = sb be head and shoulders above others
   = sb be among the best
   = sb rise above the common herd
   = sb tower above/over others

3. **Verb + Noun** entail a fierce competition　涉及激烈競爭
   = include a cut-throat competition
   = contain an intense competition
   = encompass a stiff competition
   = comprise a keen competition
   = implicate a severe competition

4. be aimed at V-ing　目的是……
   = be intended to V

5. **Verb + Noun** outshine others　勝過其他人
= outdo others
= outstrip others
= outperform others
= outrun others
= outscore others
= eclipse others
= outweigh others
= overshadow others

6. **Verb + Noun** inculcate the spirit of... in the children　灌輸……給小孩
= instill the spirit of... in the children
= implant the spirit of... in the children

7. **Verb + Noun** apply oneself　努力
= extend oneself
= make an all-out effort
= strive to VR
= endeavor to VR
= persevere in Ving
= knuckle down
= work one's fingers to the bone
= pull out all the stops
= try the whole bag of tricks

8. **Verb + Noun** make the cut　順利晉級、通過考驗
= make the grade
= cut the mustard
= pass muster
= measure up the standard
= come up to scratch
= be up to snuff

9. Noun + Infinitive the feeling to outperform others arises
出現了想勝過其他人的感覺
= the feeling to outdo others appears
= the feeling to outstrip others occurs
= the feeling to outshine others surfaces
= the feeling to outrun others takes place
= the feeling to outscore others comes up
= the feeling to eclipse others crops up
= the feeling to outweigh others crops up
= the feeling to overshadow others crops up

10. Adj + Noun prestigious colleges 有名的大學
= well-known colleges
= famous colleges
= renowned colleges
= eminent colleges
= celebrated colleges
= distinguished colleges
= famed colleges
= reputable colleges

11. Verb + Noun get their names on the merit list 榜上有名

12. Verb + Noun be admitted into these colleges 上大學
= attend these colleges
= enter these colleges
= study at these colleges
= go to these colleges

13. **Verb + Noun + Preposition** push themselves to the limit　衝破自我極限，盡全力

14. **Verb + Noun** foster creativity　激發創意
= stimulate creativity
= develop creativity
= nurture creativity
= cultivate creativity
= encourage creativity
= further creativity
= advance creativity
= promote creativity

15. **Verb + Noun** cultivate a sense of community　發展出群體感
= encourage a sense of community
= foster a sense of community
= develop a sense of community
= nurture a sense of community

16. **Adj + Noun** a sense of shared responsibility　共同責任感
= a sense of collective responsibility
= a sense of joint responsibility

17. **Verb + Adj + Noun** clinch well-deserved victory　獲勝
= ensure deserved victory
= notch up crushing victory
= pull off landslide victory
= record overwhelming victory
= score resounding victory
= secure sweeping victory
= snatch convincing victory
= win clear-cut victory

18. **Verb + Noun** brainstorm ways 集思廣益想出方法

= come up with ways

19. **Verb + Noun** elevate their performance 提升他們的表現

= strengthen their performance

= level up their performance

20. **Verb + Noun** unlock their potential 發揮他們的潛力

= develop their potential

= exploit their potential

心得筆記

Day 21   Work

The number of people working from home has grown in some countries.

What advantages and disadvantages can come to this trend?

大綱式寫作步驟解析

1. 閱讀題目，劃出分歧（破解題目）：

What **advantages** and **disadvantages** can come to this trend?

* 分歧點：advantages vs. disadvantages

2. 擬定大綱，確定結構：

第一段 : While **advantages, disadvantages**

第二段 : **advantages**

第三段 : **disadvantages**

第四段 : paraphrase your thesis

3. 參考範文／網路文章，找出論點：

2nd paragraph	
Subject:	advantages
Argument:	striking a balance between family/work + leading a healthy life
Supporting Ideas:	a. save tons of hours to do meaningful things 　　← the elimination of the daily commute 　　those who work remotely: 　　have more flexibility to juggle their personal + 　　professional responsibilities 　　→ work flexible hours + do a job with more efficacy b. getting to and from work 　　(1) wastes considerable time 　　(2) raises increased levels of stress and anxiety 　　(3) exacerbates air pollutions 　　← harmful, toxic emissions from vehicles 　　teleworking at home 　　(1) pollution is drastically reduced 　　(2) contributing to a healthy life

3rd paragraph	
Subject:	disadvantages
Argument:	low productivity + motivation
Supporting Ideas:	a. although people may have more time with loved ones → the flipside means less opportunity with colleagues challenging: collaborating with only a computer + without face-to-face connection + communication e.g., when problems arise, X (1) exchange information (2) build a rapport with others (3) getting instant support (4) address the problems b. from manager supervision to self-management: the communication between supervisors + remote workers via digital messages can go unnoticed easily (1) Keeping track of the progress becomes an issue (2) further risks achieving the desired business outcomes

4. 看著大綱，完成文章。

Traditionally, people used to travel to workplaces to do their jobs. However, the past few years have [1]**witnessed an enormous growth of** employees who work from home using computers and the Internet due to the Covid-19 pandemic. Whereas some argue that it [2]**is conducive to people's productivity**, I think this new work method also results in some drawbacks.

On the one hand, telecommuting is advantageous in [3]**striking a balance between family and work** as well as leading a healthy life. First of all, people can [4]**save tons of hours** to do meaningful things because of [5]**the elimination of the daily commute**. However, those who [6]**work remotely** have more flexibility to [7]**juggle their personal and professional responsibilities**. This helps them [8]**work flexible hours** and do a job with more efficacy. Secondly, getting to and from work every day [9]**wastes considerable time**, [10]**raises increased levels of stress and anxiety**, and most importantly [11]**exacerbates air pollution** due to harmful, toxic emissions from vehicles when people commute to their workplaces. By teleworking at home, the pollution is drastically reduced, thereby contributing to a healthy life.

On the other hand, the negative impacts on productivity should not be underestimated, especially the negative impacts on productivity and performance. Firstly, although people may have more time with loved ones when working from home, the flip side means less opportunity for face-to-face time with colleagues. [12]**Collaborating with only a computer** and without [13]**face-to-face connection** and communication can be really challenging. For example, when [14]**problems arise**, they [15]**have difficulty** exchanging information, [16]**building a rapport with others**, getting instant support, and most importantly addressing the problems. Secondly, when the management changes from manager supervision to self-management, the communication between supervisors and remote workers is conducted via digital messages, which can go unnoticed easily. [17]**Keeping track of the progress**, thus, becomes an issue and further [18]**risks achieving the desired business outcomes**.

In conclusion, working from home has its own [19]**pros and cons**. The crux is whether the employees can manage themselves efficiently and [20]**beware of** the shortcomings caused by working from home. (341 words)

加分的 Collocations

1. Verb + Noun witness an enormous growth　有大幅度成長
= see an exponential growth of

2. Adj + Preposition be conducive to...　對……有幫助
= be helpful to people's productivity
= be encouraging to people's productivity
= be advantageous to people's productivity

3. Verb + Noun + Preposition strike a balance between　取得平衡
= achieve a balance between
= create a balance between
= find a balance between
= keep a balance between
= maintain a balance between
= sustain a balance between

4. Verb + Noun save tons of hours　節省很多時間
= conserve lots of time

5. Noun + Preposition + Noun the elimination of the daily commute
　　　　　　　　　　　　　　去掉每日通勤（時間）
= the removal of the daily commute

6. Verb + Adv work remotely　遠距上班
= work distantly

7.　**Verb + Noun** juggle their personal and professional responsibilities
　　　　　　　　同時應付個人以及專業責任

8.　**Verb + Adv** work flexible hours　工時彈性
＝　work flexibly

9.　**Verb + Noun** waste considerable time　浪費大量時間
＝　fritter considerable time away

10.　**Verb + Adj + Noun** raise increased levels of stress and anxiety　增加壓力與焦慮
＝　increase high levels of stress and anxiety

11.　**Verb + Noun** exacerbate air pollution　惡化空氣汙染
＝　worsen air pollution
＝　aggravate air pollution

12.　**Verb + Preposition + Noun** collaborate with only a computer　只有和電腦合作
＝　cooperate with only a computer
＝　work together with only a computer

13.　**Adj + Noun** face-to-face connection　面對面溝通
＝　face-to-face communication

14.　**Noun + Verb** problems arise　問題出現
＝　problems occur
＝　problems happen
＝　problems come up

15.　**Verb + Noun** have difficulty + Ving　做……有困難
＝　have trouble + Ving
＝　have problems + Ving
＝　have a hard time + Ving

16. **Verb + Noun** build a rapport with...　與……建立情誼

= develop a rapport with others

= establish a rapport with others

17. **Verb + Noun + Preposition** Keep track of the progress　追蹤進度

= record the progress

= pay attention to the progress

18. **Verb + Noun** risk achieving the desired business outcomes
　　　　　冒著想要達成的結果無法達成的風險

= run the risks of achieving the desired business outcomes

= take the risks of achieving the desired business outcomes

19. pros and cons　優缺點

= advantages and disadvantages

= merits and demerits

= benefits and drawbacks

20. **Verb + Preposition** beware of　注意

= be aware of

= take heed of

Day 22　Art

For a long time, art has been considered an essential part of all cultures in the world. However, nowadays people's values have changed, and we tend to consider science, technology and business more important than arts.

What do you think are the causes of this?

What can be done to draw people's attention to art?

大綱式寫作步驟解析

1. 閱讀題目，劃出分歧（破解題目）：

What do you think are the **causes** of this?

What can be done to **draw people's attention** to art?

* **分歧點**：causes vs. draw people's attention to art

2. 擬定大綱，確定結構：

第一段：While **causes, draw people's attention to art**

第二段：**causes**

第三段：**draw people's attention to art**

第四段：paraphrase your thesis

3. 參考範文／網路文章，找出論點：

2nd paragraph	
Subject:	causes
Argument:	increasing job opportunities + the demand for latest medical facilities
Supporting Ideas:	a. science, technology + business are highly relevant to people's career advancements 　　← majors in computer science are more likely to land a well-paid job 　　a report published by International Labour Organization: an engineer gets a 25% more salary payment b. surging demand for latest medical facilities shifted our focus on the research + development 　　→ highlights + increases the desperate need for the talents involved e.g. coronavirus pandemic 　　→ in the immediate, pressing need of novel vaccines + medications (1) eradicate the disease (2) lift the whole world out of the tough times

3rd paragraph	
Subject:	solution: rekindle people's interest in art
Argument:	incorporate art in children's school curriculum + incentivizing / subsidizing artists
Supporting Ideas:	a. incorporate art in children's school curriculum: → the plants of art have been planted in every child from the early years ← take field trips to art museums or galleries (1) appreciate the works of art in person (2) know about their heritages and traditional values b. governments invest (1) by incentivizing + subsidizing artists to produce more masterpieces (2) by creating more art-related jobs → artists are more motivated to perfect their artworks → the public also will pay more attention ← can really make a living out of art

4. 看著大綱，完成文章。

For years, art has been seen [1]**an indispensable part of** culture, but this belief has been changed by [2]**the growing importance of** science, technology, and business. While there are the possible reasons for this trend, I think there are some [3]**plausible solutions to** [4]**hooking people's attention to art.**

Students have been more interested in science, technology and business—with less interest in art—owing to increasing job opportunities in modern industries. That is, these subjects [5]**are highly relevant to** people's [6]**career advancements** because graduates who major in computer science, for example, are more likely to [7]**land a well-paid job** than art students. According to a report published by International Labour Organization, an engineer gets a 25% more salary payment compared to that of an artist. Moreover, the surging demand for latest medical facilities has also [8]**shifted our focus on** the research and development, which in turn highlights and increases [9]**the desperate need for** the talents involved. A clear case in point is the recent coronavirus pandemic, which has proved to the entire world that we are in the immediate, pressing need of novel vaccines and medications to [10]**survive the crisis,** [11]**eradicate the disease** and [12]**lift the whole world out of the tough times.**

However, despite the aforementioned shift, there are still several ways to [13]**rekindle people's interest in art.** The first step is to [14]**incorporate art in children's school curriculum.** This integration would ensure that [15]**the seeds of art have been planted in** every child from early years. When they [16]**take field trips** to art museums or galleries, they can [17]**appreciate the works of art** in person and help them know about their heritages and traditional values. Another method is that governments should invest more either by [18]**incentivizing and subsidizing artists** to produce more masterpieces or by creating more art-related jobs. By so doing, not only are artists more motivated to perfect their artworks, but the public will also pay more attention to this field more because artists can really [19]**make a living** out of art.

In conclusion, although the importance of art in people's eyes [20]**pale in comparison with** the benefits offered by science, technology and business, I think if governments create more job opportunities, increase funding for artists, and combine art with school curriculum, it is still possible to draw people's attention back to art. (384 words)

加分的 Collocations

1. **Adj + Noun** an indispensable part of　不可或缺的一部份
= an imperative part of
= a vital part of
= a necessary part of
= an essential part of
= a key part of

2. **Adj + Noun** the growing importance of　越來越重要的……
= the increasing importance of
= the rising importance of
= the mounting importance of

3. **Adj + Noun** plausible solutions to + Ving　針對……的可行辦法
= feasible solutions to
= practical solutions to
= realistic solutions to
= viable solutions to
注意：此時的 to 是介系詞。

4. **Verb + Noun** hook people's attention to art　吸引人們對藝術的注意
= attract people's attention to art
= call people's attention to art
= capture people's attention to art
= catch people's attention to art
= command people's attention to art
= draw people's attention to art
= grab people's attention to art

5. **Adv + Adj** be highly relevant to...　與……高度相關
= be especially relevant to
= be extremely relevant to
= be particularly relevant to
= be very relevant to

6. **Noun + Noun** career advancements　職涯發展
= career path
= career growth
= career trajectory

7. **Verb + Noun** land a well-paid job　得到一份待遇不錯的工作
= find a highly-paid job
= find a decent job

8. **Verb + Noun** shift one's focus on...　將焦點轉移到……
= change our focus on
= transfer our focus on
= alter our focus on
= adjust our focus on

9. **Adj + Noun** the desperate need for　迫切的需求
= the burning need for
= the compelling need for
= the critical need for
= the crying need for
= the dire need for
= the driving need for
= the immediate need for
= the pressing need for
= the urgent need for

10. **Verb + Noun** survive the crisis　度過危機

11. **Verb + Noun** eradicate the disease　消滅疾病

= stamp out the disease

= wipe out the disease

= eliminate the disease

= exterminate the disease

12. **Verb + Noun** lift the whole world out of the tough times　拯救全世界幸免於難

= save the whole world out of the tough times

= rescue the whole world out of the tough times

= salvage the whole world out of the tough times

= help the whole world out of the tough times

13. **Verb + Noun** rekindle one's interest in...　再次點燃某人對……的興趣

= kindle people's interest in art

= arouse people's interest in art

= attract people's interest in art

= awaken people's interest in art

= caught people's interest in art

= drum up people's interest in art

= excite people's interest in art

= generate people's interest in art

= spark people's interest in art

= stimulate people's interest in art

= stir up people's interest in art

= whip up people's interest in art

14. **Verb + Noun** incorporate A in/into B　將 A 融入 B

= integrate art in children's school curriculum

= include art in children's school curriculum

= combine art in children's school curriculum

15. Noun + Verb | the seeds of art have been planted in

藝術的種子已經被埋入心中了

= the seeds of art have been sowed in

16. Verb + Noun | take field trips　校外教學

= go on a field trip

17. Verb + Noun | appreciate the works of art　欣賞藝術品

18. Verb + Noun | incentivize and subsidize artists　鼓勵以及資助藝術家

= encourage and fund artists

19. Verb + Noun | make a living　過活

= earn a living

= bring home the bacon

20. A pale in comparison with B　與 B 相比，A 相形見絀

= pale by comparison with

= pale into insignificance compared to

= pale beside/next to something

= put someone/something in/into the shade

= throw someone/something in/into the shade

= be inferior by comparison

= be dwarfed by something

Day 23　Housing

In some countries, people prefer to rent a house for accommodation, while in other countries people prefer to buy their own property.

Does renting a house have more advantages or disadvantages than buying a house?

⟮ 大綱式寫作步驟解析 ⟯

1. 閱讀題目，劃出分歧（破解題目）：

Does renting a house have more **advantages** or **disadvantages** than buying a house?

* **分歧點**：advantages vs. disadvantages

2. 擬定大綱，確定結構：

第一段：While **advantages, disadvantages**

第二段：**advantages**

第三段：**disadvantages**

第四段：paraphrase your thesis

3. 參考範文／網路文章，找出論點：

2nd paragraph	
Subject:	owning a home
Argument:	no maintenance costs + down payment
Supporting Ideas:	a. no maintenance costs: their landlord shoulders the whole responsibility for (1) maintenance (2) improvement (3) repairs an appliance stops working / the roof starts to leak → call the landlord to fix / replace it b. the exemption of up-front cost: renters pay a security deposit = one month's rent this deposit will be returned ← the rental property has not been damaged ⇔ a down payment > a rental security deposit $200,000 * 20% = $40,000 No money for a down payment → have no choice but to rent a house

3rd paragraph	
Subject:	owning a house
Argument:	create their dream house + a long-term investment + pride
Supporting Ideas:	a. create their dream house: tenants X renovate their property w/o landlords' permission ⇕ a complete creative freedom of creation from altering fixtures to full remodels b. owning a home = build wealth e.g. the average price of homes sold in the US ↑ 10% (2014 - 2019) Covid-19 driving the marketplace → those increases will continue c. pride: X all about \$ the pride (owning a home) would be at the top ← a home solidifies one's future + shapes most purposeful life → intangible benefits (1) a sense of stability (2) belonging to a community (3) pride of ownership

4. 看著大綱，完成文章。

It is true that many people prefer to live in a rented property because they are not responsible for [1]**miscellaneous expenses**. However, although living in a rental place has some advantages, owning a house brings more advantages.

Undoubtedly, owning a home is [2]**a lifelong goal** for many people, but renting also has its advantages: no maintenance costs and down payment. One of the benefits of renting a home is no maintenance costs or repair bills, meaning that when people rent a property, their landlord [3]**shoulders the whole responsibility for** all maintenance, improvement, and repairs. For example, if an appliance stops working or the roof starts to leak, they just call the landlord to fix or replace it. The other benefit is [4]**the exemption of up-front cost**. Renters generally have to [5]**pay a security deposit** that [6]**is equal to one month's rent**, and that is all. This deposit will be returned to them when they move out, provided the rental property has not been damaged. However, the amount for a down payment [7]**is significantly higher than** a rental security deposit. For instance, a 20% down payment on a house with a market value of $200,000 is $40,000. Thus, those unable to afford the down payment [8]**have no choice but to** rent a house.

Nonetheless, owning a house also creates some advantages tenants cannot obtain. First, people can create their dream house. As tenants, people cannot [9]**renovate their property** without [10]**landlords' permission**. Conversely, owning a home means a complete creative freedom of creation from [11]**altering fixtures** to full remodels. Second, owning a house is a smart way to [12]**build wealth**. For example, the average price of real estate sold in the United States rose 10% from 2014 to 2019. With Covid-19 driving the marketplace, those increases will continue. Finally, the benefits of owning a home are not all about money. If they are ranked [13]**in order of importance**, the pride that accompanies owning a home would be [14]**at the top** because a home [15]**solidifies one's future** and shapes most purposeful life with [16]**intangible benefits**, such as [17]**a sense of stability** and [18]**belonging to a community**. People can [19]**eliminate uncertainties** and create [20]**lasting memories** if they purchase their property.

To conclude, renting a house may lead to some advantages, but owning a house can bring more benefits that cannot be gained by a tenants. (390 words)

加分的 Collocations

1. **Adj + Noun** miscellaneous expenses　各式各樣的花費
  = assorted expenses
  = diverse expenses
  = various expenses

2. **Adj + Noun** a lifelong goal　一生的目標
  = a lifetime target

3. **Verb + Noun + Preposition** shoulder the whole responsibility for　承擔全部責任
  = assume the whole responsibility for
  = bear the whole responsibility for
  = take (on/over) the whole responsibility for

4. **Noun + Preposition + Noun** the exemption of up-front cost　沒有頭期款的成本
  = the exemption of down payment
  = the exemption of front money
  = up-front cost is exempted

5. **Verb + Noun** pay a security deposit　付訂金
  = pay an earnest money

6. **Verb + Noun** be equal to one month's rent　等於一個月的月租
  = equal one month's rent
  = be equivalent to one month's rent

7. **Adv + Adj** be significantly higher than　高於相當多

= be considerably higher than

= be substantially higher than

= be much higher than

8. **Verb + Noun** have no choice/option but to V　只能做……

= be obliged to rent a house

= be forced to rent a house

9. **Verb + Noun** renovate their property　重新裝潢房子

= renew their property

= refurbish their property

= remodel their property

= redecorate their property

10. **所有格 + Noun** landlords' permission　房東的允許

= property-owners' consent

= property-owners' authorization

= property-owners' agreement

= property-owners' approval

11. **Verb + Noun** alter fixtures　改變房子的固定設備

= change fixtures

12. **Verb + Noun** build wealth　累積財富（資產）

= accumulate wealth

= accumulate equity

13. **Preposition + Noun + Preposition** in order of importance　以重要性排序

= in sequence of importance

= in rank of importance

14. **Preposition + Noun** at the top　排名最前面

= at the peak

15. **Verb + Noun** solidify one's future　鞏固未來

16. **Adj + Noun** intangible benefits　無形的優點

= invisible advantages

= hidden advantages

17. **Noun + Preposition + Noun** a sense of stability　穩定感

= a feeling of steadiness

18. **Noun + Preposition + Noun** belonging to a community　社區歸屬感

= attachment to a community

19. **Verb + Noun** eliminate uncertainties　消除不確定性

= remove uncertainties

= resolve uncertainties

= put an end to uncertainties

20. **Adj + Noun** lasting memories　永存的記憶

= abiding memories

= enduring memories

= lingering memories

CHAPTER

5

再多 7 天，
讓你提升到 Band 7 的加分句型

再多 7 天，讓你提升到 Band 7 的加分句型

還記得評分標準的第四項 Grammatical Range and Accuracy 嗎？意思是考官會檢查你的句子結構……等，如果你能夠：

- **使用不同的句型。**

- **……**

仔細看看下面表格中的粗體字，都是表示考生有寫出「**不同的句型變化**」。也就是想要 6 分以上，就要有句型變化。反觀 5 分的評語： uses only a limited range of structures，意思是只有寫出少數的句型。

Band 5	uses only a limited range of structures
Band 6	uses a mix of simple and complex sentence forms
Band 7	uses a variety of complex structures
Band 8	uses a wide range of structures

因此，這個單元特別獨立出來要來加強你 **Grammatical Range and Accuracy** 的分數，寫出令考官驚豔的句型。此單元整理了必備的 10 種不同類型的句型：

Day 24	開頭句	+	結尾句
Day 25	因果句型	+	強調句
Day 26	轉折句型	+	讓步句型
Day 27	舉例句型	+	平行結構
Day 28	複句	+	複合句
Day 29	倒裝句		
Day 30	虛主詞句型		

Day 24　開頭句 + 結尾句

A. 開頭句

開頭句是指在第一段開場的時候可以使用的句型。第一段包含兩樣元素：**開場白 +
主旨句**。

第一段	1. 開場白：改寫題目
	2. 主旨句：回答題目

1. 開場白句型：

(1) It is + (Adv) + Adj + that...

It is indisputable that the Internet occupies an essential, irreplaceable role in
people's lives today.

（**無庸置疑的是**，網路在現今人類的生活扮演很重要且無法取代的角色。）

It is widely acknowledged that modern technology makes our world more
connected, diverse, and entertaining than ever before.

（**大家都認同的是**，現代科技讓我們的世界跟以前比起來，變得更加有連結、
更多元、且更有趣。）

It is commonly believed that education offers us more opportunities to land a
decent job and achieve better quality of life.

（**大家都認為**，教育給予我們更多機會可以找到一份好工作跟有更好的生活
品質。）

(2) There is no doubt/There is no denying that...　不可否認的是……

　　There is no doubt that the government is responsible for the safety of citizens.

　　（**不可否認的是**，政府要負起市民安全的責任。）

　　There is no denying that the accommodation problem is getting worse in big cities.

　　（**不可否認的是**，住宿問題在大城市越來越嚴重了。）

(3) An increasing/growing number of...　越來越多的……

　　An increasing number of parents realize that their children need more privacy.

　　（**越來越多的**父母親意識到小孩需要更多隱私。）

　　A growing number of children prefer to spend their free time indoors. The reason... is that...

　　（**越來越多的**小孩空閒時間比較喜歡在室內活動。原因是……。）

(4) The reason... is that...　……的原因是……

　　The reason people feel more stressed nowadays **is that** they live in a more competitive society, which requires them to work much harder than before to achieve the same results.

　　（越來越多的人在現今覺得更有壓力**的原因是**，他們處於一個更競爭的社會，這表示需要他們要比以前更加努力工作才能達到相同結果。）

(5) There is a hot debate over...　……的討論相當熱烈

　　There is a hot debate over whether women should have the same roles as men in the army.

　　（女生是否在軍中要跟男生扮演相同角色**的討論相當熱烈**。）

2. 主旨句

(1) **However, I cannot entirely agree with the idea that** traditional music is more important than modern, international music.
（**然而**，傳統音樂比現代國際音樂更重要這樣的觀點，**我無法完全同意。**）

(2) **As far as I am concerned, I agree that** money for art projects should come from both governments and other sources.
（**就我看來，我同意**藝術專案的錢應該來自於政府以及其他來源。）

(3) **Before giving my opinion, I think it is essential to** look at the argument of both sides.
（**在給出我的觀點之前，我想有必要**看看雙方的論據）

(4) **My argument for this view goes as follows.**
（我對這個問題的看法如下。）

(5) **To be frank, I cannot agree with their opinion for the reasons below.**
（坦率地說，我不能同意他們的意見，理由如下。）

B. 結尾句型

1. **From what has been discussed above, we may conclude that** the biggest factor affecting people's shopping habits is not their age group but their income level.
（**從上述討論的內容來看，我們可以總結出**影響人們購物習慣的最大因素不是年紀而是收入多寡。）

2. **For the reasons mentioned above, it seems to me that** students are more likely to be successful in their careers if they continue their studies.
（從**上述提出的原因來看，對我來說**，假如學生繼續上大學，更有可能在他們的工作方面成功。）

3. **In conclusion, while** punishments can help to prevent bad driving, **I believe that** other road safety measures should also be introduced.

（**總而言之，雖然**罰則可以避免不良駕駛，**但是我認為**其他道路安全措施應該也應採用。）

4. **Therefore, we have the reason to believe that** it would be wrong to ban testing on animals for vital medical research until equally effective alternatives have been developed.

（**因此，我們有理由相信**，為了重要的醫學研究而禁止動物測試是錯誤的，除非研發出有同樣效力的替代方案。）

5. **From my point of view, it would be better if** everyone should be able to study the course of their choice

（**在我看來**，如果每個人都能夠選擇他們喜歡的課程就讀，**也許會更好**。）

心得筆記

Day 25　因果句型 + 強調句

在英文學術寫作，作者必須清楚證明自己的論點。想要做到此點，作者就必須詳細解釋才能說服讀者他的論點是正確的。因此，因果關係的前後才是作者真正想表達的重點。

例如：**專家研究發現，改善視力模糊最佳的方式就是結婚**，因為，婚後就可以看清對方了。

A. 因果句型

1. Profits have declined **as a result of / because of / due to / owing to / thanks to / on account of** the recent drop in sales.

 = **As a result of / because of / due to / owing to / thanks to / on account of** the recent drop in sales, profits have declined.
 （**由於**最近銷售量下滑，利潤下降了。）

2. Patients were discharged from hospital **because** the beds were needed by other people.

 = **Because** the beds were needed by other people, patients were discharged from hospital.
 （**因為**急需病床，所以有些病人被要求出院。）

3. This research is important **in that** it confirms the link between aggression and alcohol.

 = This research is important **because** it confirms the link between aggression and alcohol.
 （這項研究非常重要，**因為**它證實了攻擊行為和酗酒之間的關聯。）

4. I deliberately didn't have lunch **so (that)** I would be hungry tonight.
 （我刻意不吃午飯，**為的就是**讓自己今晚能感到饑餓。）
 * 補充：**此處的** that **可以省略。**

5. She spoke **so** quietly **that** I could hardly hear her.
 （她說話**太小聲了**，**所以**我幾乎聽不到她的聲音。）
 * 補充：so + Adv + that **字面上是「如此……以至於」，實際上也表示「因果」關係。**

6. The new machines caused **such** problems **that** the company had to stop using them.
   （新機器造成了**這些**問題，**以至於**公司不得不停止使用它們。）
* 補充：such + N + that 字面上是「如此……以至於」，實際上也表示「因果」關係。

7. This box is **too** heavy **to** be carried by a little boy.
   = This box is **so** heavy **that** it can't be carried by a little boy.
   （這個箱子**太重了**，**以至於**一個小男生扛不了的。）
* 補充：too + Adj + to VR 字面上是「太……以至於無法……」，實際上也表示「因果」關係。

8. Nearly one fifth of all the electricity is produced **by** turbines spun **by** the power of falling water.
   （幾乎 1/5 的電是**由**落下的水流轉動渦輪所產生的。）
* 補充：此時的 by 文法上是被動式，但是後面加上的內容也可視為「方式、原因」。

9. What **made** you change your mind?
   （什麼**使**你改變了想法？）
* 補充：此時 make 的語意就等於 cause，因此可以視為因果關係。

10. **Once** you've signed, you won't be able to cancel the contract.
    （**一旦**你簽了字就不能解除合約了。）

11. **To succeed** in your chosen field, you must be determined.
    （**想要**在你選擇的領域上成功，你必須意志堅定。）

12. **(In order) to** make the company viable, it will unfortunately be necessary to reduce staffing levels.
    （很遺憾，**為**使公司繼續運轉下去，將不得不裁員。）

13. Most heart attacks **are caused by** blood clots.
    = Most heart attacks **are triggered by** blood clots.
    = Most heart attacks **are brought on by** blood clots.
    （大多數心臟病發作**都是由於**血栓所致。）

14. After years of research, scholars have finally **ascribed** this anonymous play **to** Shakespeare.

= After years of research, scholars have finally **attributed** this anonymous play **to** Shakespeare.

（經過多年研究，學者們終於認定這部佚名劇作是**出自**莎士比亞的手筆。）

15. Ray Charles **is largely credited for** creating soul music.

（開創靈魂樂曲風要**歸功於** Ray Charles。）

16. This grave problem **stems from** her difficult childhood.

= This grave problem **arises from** her difficult childhood.

= This grave problem **derives from** her difficult childhood.

（這個嚴重的問題主要**是因為**她艱苦的童年生活所造成的。）

17. Jack **puts** his success **(all) down to** his hard work.

（Jack 把成功**歸功於**他自身的努力。）

18. Last month's bad weather **was responsible for** the crop failure.

= Last month's bad weather **resulted in** / **led to** / **brought about** / **gave rise to** / **engendered** / **contributed to** the crop failure.

（農作物歉收**是因為**上個月天氣惡劣。）

19. Secrecy **breeds** distrust.

= Secrecy **causes** / **gives rise to** distrust.

（保有祕密**會產生**不信任。）

20. His broken leg is **the direct result of** his own carelessness.

（他自己的粗心大意直接**導致**他摔斷了腿。）

21. The accident was the inevitable **consequence** of carelessness.

= The accident was the inevitable **ramification** of carelessness.

（這場意外就是粗心的**後果**。）

22. Pills for seasickness often **induce** drowsiness.

= Pills for seasickness often **cause** drowsiness.

（暈船藥經常會**令人**昏昏欲睡。）

23. Our success **is contingent upon** your financial support.

= Our success **depends on** / **relies on** / **rests on** your financial support.

（我們的成功**有賴於**你的財務支持。）

24. We were unable to get funding and **therefore** had to abandon the project.

= We were unable to get funding and **hence** / **thus** had to abandon the project.

（我們無法籌到資金，**因此**不得不放棄計劃。）

25. The anti-smoking campaign **had had / made quite an impact on** young people.

（禁煙運動**造成年輕人很大的影響**。）

26. Diets that are high in saturated fat clog up our arteries, **thereby** reducing the blood flow to our hearts.

（高飽和脂肪的飲食容易阻塞我們的動脈，**因而**減少向心臟的供血。）

27. **With** the news that no aid would be arriving that week, hopes were dashed in the war-torn capital.

（知道那一週所有不會有救援抵達，遭受戰火蹂躪首都的人們希望都破滅了。）

＊補充：**此時的 with 有暗指因果關係的語意。**

28. **There are several reasons for** why saving minority languages could be seen as a waste of money, **but in general, they come down to three major ones.**

（對於**為何**拯救少數語言被視為浪費錢的有幾個原因，**但一般來說，可以歸結為三個主要原因。**）

29. **There are many factors that can account for** why artists should rely on alternative sources of financial support, **but the following are the most typical ones.**

（有許多原因能夠**解釋為何**藝術家應該依靠其他替代來源支助其財務，**但以下是最典型的因素。**）

30. **The reasons why** people believe that universities should only offer subjects that will be useful in the future **are as follows.**

（人們認為大學應該只提供對將來有用處的科目，**其原因如下。**）

B. 強調句

強調句是用來加強語氣，主要目的是強調句中的某個部分。被強調的部分若是指人，則可用 who 或者 whom 來代替 that。要強調的部分放在 be 動詞之後和 that 之前，再將剩下的部分放在 that 後面。此句型中，It 屬於虛主詞，本身不具任何意義，作用是將句子的結構改變；be 動詞則隨原句改變時態。所強調的部分可以**主詞**、**受詞**、**副詞**等。翻譯時，可在被強調部分之前加上**「就是，正是」**來表示強調。

強調句：It is ＋ 強調的單位（名詞／副詞）＋ that ＋ 子句

E.g. I visited Steve with Iris last night.
  → It was **I** that visited Steve with Iris last night.　（強調主詞 **I**）
  → It was **Steve** that I visited with Iris last night.　（強調受詞 **Steve**）
  → It was **with Iris** that I visited Steve last night.　（強調介詞片語 **with Iris**）
  → It was **last night** that I visited Steve with Iris.　（強調副詞 **last night**）

(1) The white dog attacked the small boy.

→ **It was** the white dog **that** attacked the small boy.

（**就是**那隻白狗攻擊那位小男生的。）

＊說明：**強調主詞** The white dog。

→ **It was** the small boy **that** the white dog attacked.

= It was the small boy whom the white dog attacked.

＊說明：**強調受詞** the small boy。**此時的** that 可以改成 whom。

(2) After Armani did his military service, he found his true calling, fashion.

→ **It was** after Armani did his military service **that** he found his true calling, fashion.

（**就在** Armani 退伍之後，他發現到他的想從事的職業：時尚業。）

＊說明：**強調副詞子句** After Armani did his military service。

(3) Because of inclement weather, the football match had to be put off.

→ **It was** because of inclement weather **that** the football match had to be put off.

（**就是**因為天氣惡劣，足球比賽被迫延後。）

＊說明：**強調介系詞片語** Because of inclement weather。

✏️ 心得筆記

Day 26 轉折句型 + 讓步句型

A. 轉折句型

轉折是一個主題換到另一個主題之間的轉變，可以藉由轉折詞來呈現，而且使語句前後的邏輯流暢表達。更重要的是，通常轉折語才是作者真正想要表達的重點。

例如：我老婆不在家，家裡的地板沒人刷、碗沒人洗、衣服沒人洗，但是，她一回來，裡裡外外的家務我馬上都做得乾淨俐落。有時候，我就是欠人監督。

1. We must not complain about the problem, **but** help to put it right.
   （我們不應該抱怨問題，**而是**應該幫助解決問題。）

2. It's a small car, **yet** it's surprisingly spacious.
   （這是一台小車，**但是**車裡相當寬敞。）

3. I thought you said the film was exciting. **On the contrary,** I nearly fell asleep halfway through it!
   （你不是說這齣電影很精彩嗎？結果**剛好相反**，看到一半我差點睡著！）

4. The couple want to eat out at a fancy restaurant, but **on the other hand** they should be saving money.
   （那對夫妻想在外面的高級餐廳吃飯，**但**他們其實應該要省錢的。）

5. He didn't reply. **Instead**, he turned on his heel and left the room.
   （他沒有回答。**相反地**，他轉身離開房間了。）

6. **Instead of** complaining, why don't we try to change things?
   （**與其**抱怨，不如我們來做一些改變？）

7. **Unexpectedly**, the demand for water is not rising as rapidly as some predicted.
（**出乎預料的是**，水的需求並非如某些人先前的預測，上升得那麼快。）

8. **Unfortunately**, I didn't have my credit card with me, or else I would have bought that bag.
（**很不湊巧**，我沒帶信用卡，否則我肯定早買那個包包了。）

9. **Fortunately**, no one was in the building when it collapsed.
（**幸好**，建築物倒塌時沒有人在裡面。）

10. **Ironically**, although many items are now cheaper to make, fewer people can afford to buy them.
（**諷刺的是**，雖然很多物品的製作成本如今下降了，但很少人買得起。）

11. Jack spent months negotiating for a pay increase, **only to** resign from his job soon after he'd received it.
（Jack 花了很長時間協商要求提高工資，**不料**工資剛提高不久就辭職了。）

12. **It turns out that** Jane had known Jack when they were children.
（**結果發現**，Jane 和 Jack 從小就認識。）

13. The truth **turned out to be** stranger than we had expected.
（**結果**，真相比我們預期的更離奇。）

14. If we served more soft drinks, there would be fewer hangovers and, **more importantly**, fewer drink-driving incidents.
（如果我們提供更多無酒精的飲料，宿醉就會比較少發生，**更重要的是**，酒駕事件就會更少。）

15. **Not only** was a monopoly of cinnamon becoming impossible, **but (also)** the spice trade overall was diminishing in economic potential, and was eventually superseded by the rise of trade in coffee, tea, chocolate, and sugar.
（肉桂壟斷**不僅僅**不可能了，**而且**香料貿易整體經濟重要性也降低了，最終因咖啡、茶、巧克力和糖的貿易崛起而被取代了。）

16. "You must be exhausted after that long journey."

"**Actually**, I feel fine."

（「走了這麼遠之後，你一定非常的疲倦。」

「**事實上**，我覺得還好。」）

17. Many people thought she was Portuguese, but **in (actual) fact** she's Brazilian.

（很多人以為她是葡萄牙人，**可是實際上**她是巴西人。）

18. The CEO seemed very young, but he was **in reality (= in fact)** older than all of us.

（那位 CEO 看上去很年輕，**可是實際上**他比我們所有人年齡都大。）

19. Hiram Bingham was ready for what was to be the greatest achievement of his life**: the exploration of Machu Picchu.**

（Hiram Bingham 準備好要來迎接他生命中最偉大的成就：**探索馬丘比丘**。）

* 補充：**此句型是同位語放句尾的結構，此時有補充說明和強調的功能。**

B. 讓步句型

1. I have the greatest respect for his ideas **although** I don't agree with him.

= **Although** / **While** / **Whereas** I don't agree with him, I have the greatest respect for his ideas.

（**雖然**我不認同他，但是我非常尊重他的想法。）

2. **Despite** / **In spite of** repeated assurances that the product is safe, many people have stopped buying it.

（**儘管**一再保證了該產品的安全性，很多人還是不再購買。）

3. **Notwithstanding** some members' objections, I think we must go ahead with the plan.

（**儘管**遭到一些成員反對，我還是認為我們應該實施該計劃。）

4. There are serious problems in our country. **Nonetheless / Nevertheless**, we feel this is a good time to return.

（我們國家存在嚴重問題。**儘管如此**，我們仍覺得這是歸國的好時機。）

5. **Even if** you take a taxi, you'll still miss your flight.

（**即使**搭計程車去，你還是趕不上班機。）

6. **Even though** he left school at 16, he still managed to become a CEO.

（**儘管**他年僅 16 歲就輟學了，但最終還是當上了 CEO。）

7. **Admittedly**, I could have tried harder but I still don't think all this criticism is fair.

（**不可否認**，我本來可以再努力些。儘管如此，我還是認為這些批評也並非完全公道。）

8. **It is true that** computers have become an essential tool for teachers and students in all areas of education.

（**的確**，電腦在所有的教育領域中，對於老師和學生來說已經變成必要的工具。）

9. An immediate interest cut might give a small boost to the economy. **Even so**, any recovery is likely to be very slow.

（立即降息或許小有促進經濟。**即使如此**，各方面的復甦可能非常緩慢。）

10. I've thought about it so much, but **even now/then** I can't believe how lucky I was to survive the accident.

（我一直在不停地想，但**儘管如此**，我還是無法相信自己怎會如此幸運，竟能在事故中死裡逃生。）

Day 27　舉例句型 + 平行結構

A. 舉例句型

1. **For example / For instance, S + V ...　舉例來說……**

   For example, air comprised mainly nitrogen and oxygen.

   = Air, **for example,** comprised mainly nitrogen and oxygen.

   = Air comprised mainly nitrogen and oxygen, **for example**.

   （**舉例來說**，空氣主要是由氮氣和氧氣組成的。）

2. **Take... for example.　以……為例**

   People love British cars. **Take** the Mini **for example**. In Japan, it still sells more than all the other British cars put together.

   （人們熱愛英國車，**以** Mini **為例**，它在日本的銷量比他牌英國車銷量的總和都要來得多。）

   * 注意：Take... for example 是祈使句，也就是一個完整的句子，因此要用句號。如果用逗號，會變成有兩個句子而少了連接詞的錯誤。

   → People love British cars. **To take** the Mini **for example**, in Japan, it still sells more than all the other British cars put together.

   * 注意：To take... for example 變成不定詞當副詞使用，所以可以用逗號，因為真正的句子是從 it 開始。

3. **A case in point is... (= ... is a case in point)　以……為例**

   Lack of good communication causes grave problems, and **a case in point** is their marriage.

   = Lack of good communication causes grave problems, and their marriage is **a case in point**.

   （缺乏良好溝通會導致嚴重問題，他們的婚姻就是個**典型的例子**。）

265

CHAPTER

5

4. **a concrete example is ...** 一個實例是⋯⋯

Let me give **a concrete example of** what I mean.

（我來**舉一個具體例子**説明我的意思。）

5. **more specifically** 更確切地來說

The newspaper, **more specifically**, the editor, was taken to court for publishing the photographs.

（這家報社，**更確切地來說是**編輯，因刊登這些照片被控告。）

6. **such as / like...** 例如⋯⋯／像是⋯⋯

Many animals, **such as / like** sheep and cows, live on the farm.

（很多動物，**像是**羊群及牛群，都住在農場裡。）

7. **namely** 就是⋯⋯

The show needs to concentrate on their target audience, **namely** men aged between 30 and 40.

（這個節目需要專注在他們的目標觀眾，**也就是**介於三十到四十歲的男性。）

8. **(let's) say (that)** 建議／比方說

Try to finish the work by, **let's say**, Thursday.

（**建議**盡量在星期四前完成這項工作。）

9. **S, including + N... , V...** 包括⋯⋯

Ten people, **including** two children, were killed in the blast.
（10 人在這起爆炸中身亡，其中**包括**兩名兒童。）

10. **... can be listed as follows** ⋯⋯可列舉如下

Generally, the advantages **can be listed as follows**.

（一般來説，其優勢**可以列舉如下**。）

B. 平行結構

平行結構表示**使用相同的句子結構和形式**，因為**類似的句子結構和形式可以讓讀者（考官）比較容易讀懂。**

平行結構常見六種類型：

1. 名詞片語

   (1) Mr. Evan is **a lawyer**, **a politician**, and **a teacher**.

   （Mr. Evan 是一位**律師**、**政治家**、也是**老師**。）

   (2) Even after the merger, our priority is to serve our main customers: **small to mid-sized businesses** and **personal customers**.

   （即使在併購後，我們的優先考慮的是要服務我們的主要客戶：**中小型企業**以及**個人戶**。）

2. 動名詞片語

   (1) Sam is responsible for **stocking merchandise**, **writing orders for delivery**, and **selling computers**.

   （Sam 負責**備貨**、**寫交貨單**、和**銷售電腦**。）

   (2) Unfortunately, our company is going through a listing process on the stock market, so most of our effort is dedicated to **creating presentations for the investors**, **discussing the joint program**, and **analyzing our company's growth over the past few years**.

   （不幸的是，我們公司正在進行上市掛牌，所以我們主要心力放在**向投資人做簡報**、**討論共同計劃**，和**分析過去幾年來的公司成長**。）

3. 不定詞片語

   (1) I did that both **to fulfill my dream** and **(to) make a profit**.

   （我這麼做是**為了實現夢想**以及**賺錢**。）

(2) When he ran for the presidency, he promised **to cut taxes, (to) solve energy shortage**, and **(to) end racism**.

（當競選總統時，他承諾要**減稅、解決能源短缺問題、終結種族歧視**。）

4. 形容詞片語

(1) Seoul is **large, crowded**, and **fascinating**.

（首爾**很大、很壅擠**和**吸引人**。）

(2) The students were **unprepared, poorly behaved**, and **disruptive**.

（這些學生**毫無準備、行為不良、又愛搗蛋**。）

5. 句子

(1) **Most of us were in the hall, the doors had been closed, and the lights were out**.

（**我們大部分的人都在大廳裡，門已上鎖，燈也熄滅了**。）

(2) **Not only** was he rude, **but** he **also** ate all the shrimp balls.

（他**不只**沒禮貌，**還**吃光了所有的蝦球。）

6. 動詞 + 副詞

(1) Anyone can write well if they learn to **think logically, organize ideas coherently**, and **express ideas clearly**.

（任何人都可以寫得很好，假如他們能夠**有邏輯地思考、有連貫地組織想法、和清楚表達想法**。）

(2) The eruption **began slowly, continued sporadically**, and **ended catastrophically**.

（火山爆發**緩緩開始、間歇性地持續、然後毀滅性地結束**。）

Day 28　複句 + 複合句

英文句子的結構基本上包含單句、合句、複句，複合句四種。熟悉這四種句構的文法，可以幫助我們寫出清晰正確的長難句。

1. 單句

任何一個五大句型的句子。

(1) That is not your business.
（不干你的事。）

(2) That traditional dish tastes good.
（這道菜嘗起來很棒）

2. 合句

由**對等連接詞（and, but, or**……**等）**合成的**兩個對等子句**。

(1) I am Patrick **and** love to teach English.
（我是 Patrick，**而且**我熱愛教英文。）

(2) We must not complain about the problem, **but** help to put it right.
（我們不應該抱怨問題，**而是**應該協助解決問題。）

3. 複句

一個**主要子句** + **從屬子句**組成。從屬子句包括**名詞子句**、**形容詞子句**、**副詞子句**。

(1) I don't know **when I can complete my third book**—*Collocation*.

（我不知道我何時可以完成我第三本書《詞語搭配》。）

* 說明：**這裡加了名詞子句** when I can complete my third book—*Collocation*。

(2) The price of the watch **which I bought** was steep.

（我之前買的手錶價格昂貴。）

* 說明：**這裡加了形容詞子句** which I bought。

(3) **When Katie came in**, Roger was **smoking**.

（當 Katie 進來時，Roger 當時正在吸菸。）

* 說明：**這裡加了副詞子句** When Katie came in。

練習：把兩個單句變成複句。

(1) The player's performance was particularly impressive.

He scored 30 points within the first half.

→ The player's performance was particularly impressive _____ he

scored 30 points within the first half.

（這位球員的表現相當令人精彩，**因為**他在上半場就得了 30 分。）

* 說明：**答案是** because，因為這兩句有「因果關係」。

(2) Food critics recommend ZJ's Bistro as the best restaurant in the area.

Most local residents prefer Dree's Café.

→ _____ food critics recommend ZJ's Bistro as the best restaurant in

the area, most residents prefer Dree's Café.

（**雖然**美食評論家推薦 ZJ 小館為此區域最棒的餐廳，但是大部分的當地人都選

擇 Dree's 咖啡廳。）

* 說明：**答案是** although，因為這兩句有「讓步關係」。

4. 複合句：複句 + 合句

(1) **When** Katie came in, R-oger was smoking **and** playing the guitar.

（**當** Katie 進來時，Roger 當時正在抽菸**和**彈吉他。）

＊說明：When Katie came in, Roger was smoking 這是由 when 引導的複句；Roger was smoking and playing the guitar 是由 and 引導的合句，所以整個合在一起稱作是「複合句」。

練習：把句子變成複合句。

(1) We should plan our trip early.

We should book our flight as soon as possible.

We have to book a room.

→We should plan our trip early _____ book our flight as soon as possible _____ we have to book a room.

（我們應該早一點計畫旅行**並且**盡快訂機票，**因為**我們還要訂房間。）

＊說明：答案是先用 and 把前兩句變成合句，再用 because 連接第三句，變成複合句。

(2) She came in the flat.

Her mother was cooking.

Her father was reading.

→_____ she came in the flat, her mother was cooking _____ her father was reading.

（**當**她進來公寓時，她媽媽當時正在煮飯**而**她爸爸正在閱讀。）

＊說明：答案是先用 When 把前兩句變成複句，再用 and 連接第三句，變成複合句。

Day 29 倒裝句

你知道為什麼要寫成倒裝句？當作者想要**「強調」**原句中的某些資訊時，會把想要強調的字句移到**句首**，因為句首位置是一個句子最顯眼的地方。

常見倒裝句分成 6 種：
1. 地方副詞 放句首
2. 否定副詞 放句首
3. 讓步句型 倒裝句
4. so... that 和 such... that
5. 準關代 as 和 than 的倒裝
6. 當補語用的形容詞、現在分詞、過去分詞

1. 地方副詞 放句首，規則如下：
　① 把**地方副詞**放在句首。
　② 把**主詞**和**動詞**的位置**互相交換**！
　③ 注意，此時動詞只能是「不及物動詞」與「be 動詞」。

(1)　*An Oxford Advanced Learners' Dictionary* is on my desk.
　　　　　　　　　　S　　　　　　　　　　V　　地方副詞

→　On my desk is an *Oxford Advanced Learners' Dictionary*.
　　地方副詞　　V　　　　　　　　S

　　（有一本牛津字典在我桌上。）

> 說明：
> ① 地方副詞 **on my desk** 移到句首。
> ② 再把主詞 An *Oxford Advanced Learners' Dictionary* 和 **be** 動詞 **is** 對調。

(2)　The tender melody of music floated within the house.
　　　　　　　　S　　　　　　　　　　Vi　　　　地方副詞

→　Within the house floated the tender melody of music.
　　（柔和的音樂旋律漂浮在屋內。）

27

> 說明：
> ①地方副詞 within the house 移到句首。
> ②再把主詞 the tender melody of music 和不及物動詞 float 對調。

CHAPTER 5

(3)　**Here** comes the bus.（公車來了。）
　　　　　　　　Vi　　　S

→　The bus comes **here**.
　　　S　　　　　Vi

> 說明：原來這句我們常講的句子也是倒裝句喔！為了突顯出「來了」，所以把地方副詞 here 移到句首來強調。
> ①地方副詞 here 移到句首。
> ②再把主詞 the bus 和不及物動詞 come 對調。

(4)　**It** is here.（它在這裡。）
→　Here **it** is.

> 說明：注意，如果主詞是「代名詞」，倒裝時，主詞和動詞不用換位置。
> ①地方副詞 here 移到句首。
> ②主詞 it 和 be 動詞 is 不用換位置。

2. 否定副詞 放句首，這種句型因為有不同動詞的緣故，所以分成兩種類型：
a. 動詞是「一般動詞」。
① 把 否定副詞 移到句首。
② 加一個 助動詞 。
③ 再把動詞變成 原形動詞 。

(1) **never**　從未

He **never** goes to the Ambassador Theaters.
　S　　　　Vi

→　**Never does** he **go** to the Ambassador Theaters.

（他**從來沒**去過國賓戲院。）

> 說明：
> ① 把 │否定副詞 never│ 移到句首。
> ② 加一個 │助動詞 does│。
> ③ 再把動詞變成 │原形動詞 go│。

(2) **hardly**　幾乎不

Andy **hardly** remembered what he did last week.
　S　　　　　　Vt

→　**Hardly did** Andy **remember** what he did last week.

（Andy **幾乎無法**記得上星期做過什麼事情了。）

> 說明：
> ① 把 │否定副詞 hardly│ 移到句首。
> ② 加一個 │助動詞 did│。
> ③ 再把動詞變成 │原形動詞 remember│。

(3) **little**　只有一點

E.g.　Many people know **little** about the hypocrite.
　　　　S　　　　Vi

→　**Little do** many people **know** about the hypocrite.

（很多人**一點都不**了解那位偽君子。）

(4) **seldom / rarely** 很少

<u>People</u> **seldom** <u>offered</u> <u>an apology</u> after they made mistakes.
    S   Vt   O

→ **Seldom did** <u>people</u> **offer** an apology after they made mistakes.
（人們犯錯後**很少**道歉。）

(5) **only** 只有

<u>You</u> <u>realize</u> its value **only** {when you lose your health}.
  S   Vt

→ **Only {when you lose your health} do** <u>you</u> **realize** its value.
（**只有**失去健康後你才會了解它的價值。）

(6) **not only... but also**　不僅僅……還有……

E.g.　He **not only** passed the exam **but also** scored at the top.
　　　　　S　　　　　　　Vt

→　**Not only did** he pass the exam but also scored at the top. (X)

　　（他**不僅僅**通過考試，**而且還是**最高分。）

說明：
① 把 否定副詞 **not only** 移到句首。
② 加一個 助動詞 **did**。
③ 再把動詞變成 原形動詞 **pass**。

注意，此時兩邊句子不對稱，因為**左邊是句子** he pass the exam，右邊是動詞片語 scored at the top。

→　Not only did he pass the exam but also **he** scored at the top. (X)

說明：因為上面的句子**不對稱**，所以**右邊的句子加上主詞** he，讓兩邊都看起來像是一個句子 he pass the exam 和 he scored at the top。但是如果我們再仔細看看，會發現右邊的句子還是有修辭學上的問題，**因為此時的副詞 also 很像是修飾 he**，但是實際上 also 不是修飾 he，而是要修飾後面的動詞片語 scored at the top。

→　Not only did he pass the exam but **he** also scored at the top. (O)

說明：因此，為了解決這個問題，我們把右邊的主詞 he 移到 but also 的中間，這樣一來，副詞 also 就緊鄰動詞片語 scored at the top，也因此解決修辭學的問題了。

快速口訣：
① 把否定副詞 **not only** 移到句首。
② 加一個**助動詞 did**。
③ 再把動詞變成原形動詞 **pass**。
④ 右邊加上主詞，並且放在 but also 中間。

b. 動詞是「**be 動詞或助動詞**」。

① 把**否定副詞**移到句首。

② 再把「**主詞和 be 動詞或助動詞**」對調。

(7) **never**　從來不

I shall **never** forget the idiom "Familiarity breeds contempt."
S　助

→　**Never shall I** forget the idiom "Familiarity breeds contempt."
助　S

（我**永遠都不會**忘記這句成語「親近生慢侮」。）

說明：
① 把 否定副詞 never 移到句首。
② 再把主詞 I 和助動詞 shall 對調。

(8) **hardly**　僅僅

Scott had **hardly** arrived home when the phone rang.
S　助

→　**Hardly had Scott** arrived home when his phone rang.
助　S

（Scott **才剛**到家電話就響了。）

說明：
① 把 否定副詞 hardly 移到句首。
② 再把主詞 Scott 和助動詞 had 對調。

(9) **little 很少**

Stella <u>might</u> know **little** about constellation and Greek mythology.
     S   助

→   **Little** <u>might</u> <u>Stella</u> know about constellation and Greek mythology.
          助   S

（Stella 可能只了解**一點點**星座與希臘神話故事。）

> 說明：
> ① 把 否定副詞 little 移到句首。
> ② 再把主詞 Stella 和助動詞 might 對調。

(10) **seldom**

<u>Environemtal issues</u> <u>have</u> **seldom** attracted so much media attention.
       S   助

→   **Seldom** <u>have</u> <u>environmental issues</u> attracted so much media attention.
          助   S

（環境議題**很少**吸引媒體的關注。）

> 說明：
> ① 把 否定副詞 seldom 移到句首。
> ② 再把主詞 environemtal issues 和助動詞 have 對調。

(11) **only 只有**

<u>People</u> <u>can</u> succeed **only** {by studying English hard}.
    S   助

→   **Only** {by studying English hard} <u>can</u> <u>people</u> succeed.
                            助   S

（**只有**認真念英文才會成功。）

説明：
① 注意，此時不是只有把 否定副詞 only 放在句首就好了，因為 only 是修飾後面的副詞子句，所以要把 only 跟後面的副詞子句視為一體，然後整個移到句首。
② 再把主詞 people 和助動詞 can 對調。

(12) **not... until** 直到……才……

<u>Tim</u> <u>did</u> **not** sleep **until five o'clock**.
　　S　　助

→　**Not until five o'clock** <u>did</u> <u>Tim</u> sleep.
　　　　　　　　　　　　　　助　　S

（Tim 到五點**才**去睡覺。）

説明：注意，此時的否定副詞 not 要視為修飾後面的副詞子句，因此移到句首倒裝時，也是要一起往前移。
① 把 否定副詞 not 和 副詞子句 until five o'clock 一起移到句首。
② 再把主詞 Tim 和助動詞 did 對調。

此外，我們可以再從上面的倒裝句變成「強調句」。

　　　Not until five o'clock <u>did</u> <u>Tim</u> sleep.

→　It was **not until five o'clock** <u>that Tim slept</u>.

説明：
① 套入 "It is/was + 要強調的內容 + that..."。
② 要強調的內容 就是否定副詞 not until five o'clock。
③ that 裡面的動詞要還原成過去式，因為原本有助動詞 did。

(13) **no sooner... than**　才……就……

The farmer <u>had</u> **no sooner** started mowing the lawn **than** it started raining.
S　　助

→　**No sooner** had <u>the farmer</u> started mowing the lawn **than** it started raining.
助　　　S

（那位農夫**才**一開始除草**就開始**下雨了。）

說明：
① 把 否定副詞 no sooner 移到句首。
② 再把主詞 the farmer 和助動詞 had 對調。

(14) **S + V（否定）... nor 助動詞／be 動詞 + S...**　不會……，也不會……

True friends **don't** ruin their friendship, **nor do they ask** for anything for it.
（真正的朋友**不會破壞友誼**，**也不會**為了友誼而要求任何回報。）

(15) 其他常見**否定副詞放句首**的倒裝句

By no means will I share my room with that guy.
（我**絕對不要**跟那個人同一間房睡覺。）

Under no circumstances should you be allowed to stay up late, since you are in poor health.
（**在任何情況下**你**都不**應該熬夜，因為你的健康狀況不好。）

On no account should the house be left unlocked.
（**在任何情況下都不**應該不鎖門。）

3. 讓步句型 的倒裝句，此時有 **3 種情況**：

(1) 當主詞補語是形容詞或名詞時：

Although <u>our country</u> <u>is</u> <u>rich</u>, the qualities of our living are not satisfactory.
S　　V　SC

→　**Rich as/though** <u>our country</u> <u>is</u>, the qualities of our living are not satisfactory.
SC　　　　　S　　V

（**雖然**我們國家很有錢，**但是**我們的生活水準一點都不令人滿意。）

說明：
① 刪除句首的 although。
② 把**主詞補語**的**形容詞** rich 移到句首。
③ 再加上 **as** 或是 **though**。

Although <u>Christina</u> <u>is</u> <u>an engineer</u>, she doesn't like programming.
　　　　　　　S　　V　　SC

→ **Engineer as/though** <u>Christina</u> <u>is</u>, she doesn't like programming.
　　SC　　　　　　　　　S　　V

（**雖然** Christina 是工程師，**但**她不喜歡寫程式。）

說明：
① 刪除句首的 although。
② 把**主詞補語**的**名詞** engineer 移到句首，**此時的名詞不加冠詞**。
③ 再加上 **as** 或是 **though**。

(2) **讓步句型的副詞**

Although <u>he</u> <u>worked</u> <u>hard</u>, he couldn't support his family.
　　　　　　 S　　Vi　　adv

→ **Hard as/though** <u>he</u> <u>worked</u>, he couldn't support his family.
　 adv　　　　　　 S　　Vi

（**雖然**他很努力工作，**但是**他還是養不了家。）

說明：
① 刪除句首的 although。
② 把**副詞** hard 移到句首。
③ 再加上 **as** 或是 **though**。

(3) **讓步句型**的動詞

Although Hunk might <u>try</u>, he still cannot defeat his opponent.
　　　　　 S　　　 V

→ **Try as** <u>Hunk</u> might, he still cannot defeat his opponent.

（**雖然** Hunk 嘗試了，**但是**他還是無法擊敗他的對手。）

> 說明：
> ① 刪除句首的 although。
> ② 把**動詞 try** 移到句首。
> ③ 再加上 **as** 或是 **though**。

4. so... that 和 such... that 的倒裝句

(1) <u>Christy</u> <u>was</u> **so** happy **that** she burst into tears.
　　 S　　 V

→ **So happy** was <u>Christy</u> that she burst into tears.
　　　　　　 V　　 S

（Christy 喜極而泣。）

> 說明：
> ① 把 so... that 和 such... that 句型的 **so happy** 視為類似**否定副詞**，然後**移到句首**。
> ② 再來把**主詞 Christy** 和 **be 動詞 was** 對調。
>
> 補充：
> so　 + Adj/Adv + that...
> such + NP　　 + that...

(2) <u>He</u> <u>works</u> **so** hard **that** he can make a fortune.
　　 S　　 Vi

→ **So hard** does he work that he can make a fortune.
（他非常努力，可以賺大錢了。）

說明：
① 把 so... that 和 such... that 句型的 **so hard** 視為類似**否定副詞**，然後**移到句首**。
② 加一個**助動詞 does**。
③ 再把動詞變成 原形動詞 work 。

(3) A kabe-don is **such** a powerful move **that** no girls can handle it.
             S   V

→ **Such a powerful move** is a kabe-don that no girls can handle it.
                               V   S

（壁咚是一個強而有力的動作，沒有女孩子招架得住。）

說明：
① 把 so... that 和 such... that 句型的 **such a powerful move** 視為類似**否定副詞**，
   然後**移到句首**。
② 再來把**主詞 a kabe-don** 和 **be 動詞 is** 對調。

5. **準關代 as** 和 **than** 的從屬子句倒裝。

(1) Chandler studies as hard as Ross.

→ Chandler studies as hard as Ross **does.**
                           S   助

→ Chandler studies as hard as **does** Ross.（倒裝句）
                          助   S

（Chandler 跟 Ross 一樣用功念書。）

說明：此句型有三種寫法：
① 省略句尾的助動詞 does。
② 把助動詞 does 寫出來。
③ 把助動詞 does 移到主詞 Ross 前面，變成倒裝句。

(2) Phoebe studies English by rote learning, as most of other students.

→ Phoebe studies English by rote learning, as <u>most of other students</u> **do**.
S 助

→ Phoebe studies English by rote learning, as **do** <u>most of other students</u>.（倒裝句）
助 S

（Phoebe 用死背的方式唸英文，就跟其他大部分的學生一樣。）

> 說明：此句型有三種寫法：
> ① 省略句尾的助動詞 do。
> ② 把助動詞 do 寫出來。
> ③ 把助動詞 do 移到主詞 most of other students 前面，變成倒裝句。

(3) I love movies more than <u>others</u>.

I love movies more than <u>others</u> <u>do</u>.
S 助

→ I love movies more than **do** <u>others</u>.（倒裝句）
助 S

（我比其他人更加熱愛電影。）

> 說明：此句型有三種寫法：
> ① 省略句尾的助動詞 do。
> ② 把助動詞 do 寫出來。
> ③ 把助動詞 do 移到主詞 others 前面，變成倒裝句。

6. 當補語用的**形容詞**、**現在分詞**、**過去分詞**也可以放句首，變成倒裝句。

(1) <u>The team who wins the World Game</u> will be **happy**.
S V SC

→ **Happy** <u>will be</u> <u>the team who wins the World Game</u>.
SC V S

（贏得世界盃的團隊將會很開心。）

說明：
①將主詞補語的形容詞 **happy** 移到句首。
②再將**主詞** the team who wins the World Game 和**動詞** will be 對調。

(2)　The attachment (confirming the news) is **enclosed**.
　　　　　　　　S　　　　　　　　　　　　　V　　Vpp

→　　**Enclosed** is the attachment (confirming the news).

（證實那項消息的檔案已經附在夾帶檔案裡面了。）

說明：
①將**過去分詞** enclosed 移到句首。
②再將**主詞** the attachment confirming the news 和**動詞** is 對調。

(3)　**Given** is [one graph (exhibiting the marked similarities between Music Choice
　　　Vpp　 V　　　　　　　　　　　　　　　　　　　　S

　　and Pop Parade on the Internet in fifteen days period of time)].

→　　[One graph (exhibiting the marked similarities between Music Choice and Pop
　　　　　　　　　　　　　　　　　　　　S

Parade on the Internet in fifteen days period of time)] is **given**.
　　　　　　　　　　　　　　　　　　　　　　　　　　　　V　　Vpp

（底下這張圖表呈現 Music Choice 和 Pop Parade 在 15 天當中的明顯相似處。）

說明：
第二句（原句）主詞和動詞距離太長了，導致結構不明確，會造成讀者閱讀
上的困難。因此，把過去分詞 given 倒裝時會比較清楚，因為修辭學上**允許
很長的單位放在後面**，也就是**尾重原則**。步驟：
①將**過去分詞** given 移到句首。
②再將**主詞** One graph⋯ time 和 be 動詞 is 對調。

Day 30 虛主詞（It）句型

1. 作虛主詞

(1) It is + 形容詞（人的特質）+（of + 人）+ to + VR

wise, smart, stupid foolish, kind, polite generous, selfish, considerate...

例：（你）打斷別人的對話是很不禮貌的。

→ **It is** rude (of you) to interrupt other people's conversation.

(2) It is + 形容詞（事／物的特性）+（for + 人）+ to + VR

easy, difficult, safe, dangerous, (im)possible, (un)necessary,

essential, crucial, important, satisfactory...

* 注意：此類形容詞非描述人，而是描述事物的特性。

例：**我們很難**完成這項艱鉅的任務。

→ **It is hard/difficult for us to** complete the Herculean/mammoth task.

2. 尾重原則

所謂的尾重原則是指結構較長的受詞，例如名詞片語、不定詞和名詞子句，會把它們放在句末，也就是句子的尾巴。

S + think, find, consider + it + N /Adj + to + VR

make, believe, regard + that + SV

deem, take, imagine

suppose, count

(1) Technology makes **our life in the outer space** possible.
　　　S　　　　Vt　　　　　　O　　　　　　　　　OC

→ Technology makes possible **our life in the outer space**.

（科技使在外太空生活變得可能。）

(2) <u>The expansion of artificial irrigation systems</u> **makes** <u>the growth of 40% of the</u>
                             S   Vt   O

<u>world's food</u> **possible**.
      OC

→   The expansion of artificial irrigation systems **makes possible** <u>the growth of 40% of the world's food</u>.

（人工灌溉系統的提升有可能使全球糧食產收增加四成。）

(3) <u>I</u> <u>think</u> **to live on the moon** <u>impossible</u>.
    S Vt   O   OC

→   I think **it** impossible **to live on the moon**.

(4) <u>I</u> <u>believe</u> **that you can pass the exam** possible.
    S Vt   O   OC

→   I believe **it** possible **that you can pass the exam**.

30 天雅思寫作 7+ 攻略：必備句型、加分搭配詞、
邏輯寫作大綱，取分重點考前完全掌握 / 蕭志億（派
老師）著 . -- 初版 . -- 臺北市：日月文化出版股份有
限公司, 2022.03
　　288 面；19×25.7 公分 . -- (EZ talk)
ISBN 978-626-7089-16-3（平裝）

1.CST: 國際英語語文測試系統　2.CST: 作文
805.189　　　　　　　　　　　　　　110021845

EZ TALK

30天雅思寫作7+攻略：
必備句型、加分搭配詞、邏輯寫作大綱，取分重點考前完全掌握

作　　　者： 蕭志億（派老師）
責 任 編 輯： 鄭莉璇、劉韋宏、許宇昇
裝 幀 設 計： 賴佳韋工作室
內 頁 排 版： 簡單瑛設
行 銷 企 劃： 張爾芸

發 行 人： 洪祺祥
副 總 經 理： 洪偉傑
副 總 編 輯： 曹仲堯
法 律 顧 問： 建大法律事務所
財 務 顧 問： 高威會計師事務所

出　　　版： 日月文化出版股份有限公司
製　　　作： EZ叢書館
地　　　址： 臺北市信義路三段151號8樓
電　　　話： (02) 2708-5509
傳　　　眞： (02) 2708-6157
網　　　址： www.heliopolis.com.tw
郵 撥 帳 號： 19716071日月文化出版股份有限公司

總 經 銷： 聯合發行股份有限公司
電　　　話： (02) 2917-8022
傳　　　眞： (02) 2915-7212

印　　　刷： 中原造像股份有限公司
初　　　版： 2022年3月
初 版 3 刷： 2023年9月
定　　　價： 380元
I S B N： 978-626-7089-16-3